'Bloody good! An eminently accessible and highly amusing look at growing up in a lower middle class family in Sydney's vast, magnificent slab of south-western suburbs.'

Reg Mombassa, Mental As Anything

'For some, the 1960s is nothing more than an acid flashback. By the time most people found themselves, there was nobody home! Not so with Moya Sayer-Jones. Her reminiscence of this decade of self-discovery is warm, whimsical, well-observed . . . and goes straight for the jocular vein.'

Kathy Lette

'Little Sister freefalls through the 1950s, 1960s and 1970s taking us through the mores, morality and changes of a Sydney family as it moves from Glebe to Bexley and as Little Sister travels her own journey from school to university and marriage.

Little Sister is a very funny book and a rich, articulate document recording the world of laminex, flares, recliners, school hats and physical culture.'

Glenda Adams

GW00712380

To Sid and Jessie
and RJN

LITTLE SISTER

MOYA SAYER-JONES

Drawings by Reg Lynch

A Susan Haynes Book
Allen & Unwin Australia

Sydney   Wellington   London   Boston

With special thanks to Susan Chenery,
Robin Powell and Susan Haynes

Written with the assistance of the Literature Board of the
Australia Council.

First published in 1988
A Susan Haynes book
Allen & Unwin Australia Pty Ltd
An Unwin Hyman company
8 Napier Street, North Sydney, NSW 2060
Australia

Allen & Unwin New Zealand Limited
60 Cambridge Terrace, Wellington
New Zealand

Unwin Hyman Limited
15–17 Broadwick Street, London WIV 1FP
England

Allen & Unwin Inc.
8 Winchester Place, Winchester, Mass 01890
USA

National Library of Australia
Cataloguing-in-publication
        Jones, Moya Sayer.
        Little sister.
        ISBN 0 04 320217 9.
        I. Title
        A823'.3

Set in Plantin by Best-set Typesetter Ltd., Hong Kong
Produced by SRM Production Services Sdn Bhd, Malaysia.

CONTENTS

1   The Move

'Moya' was a pretty unusual name for a child born in 1953. Most little girls were Susan or Elizabeth or Rhonda or Jennifer and I might have been called that too if my two older sisters hadn't beaten me to the punch. By the time I came along, Mum and Dad were drained of inspiration. Two daughters with two names each meant four good ideas already. The post-war baby boom was partly to blame. It left our family crowded with namesakes of every available relative. One aunt was still to be honoured but she had big, flashy breasts and a de facto and so was never a real consideration. I was ten days old before Mum saw a picture of an Irish tap dancer in the afternoon paper. The girl was very beautiful with long hair, slim legs and small breasts and there was no mention of extra-marital sex. Her name was Moya.

The day Mum and Dad brought me home from the hospital our street had a big party. There were streamers hanging from the electricity poles, fireworks, trestle tables covered in sandwiches and laundry boilers filled with bottled beer. Everyone was really excited. No cars were allowed in after six o'clock but this wasn't too much of a hardship for the residents because no one in the street owned one. Dad carried me in the bassinet from the bus stop. It was a long walk, winding through the trestles and shaking hands with all the people, but Dad didn't care. He said a new queen didn't arrive every day. He wasn't talking about me. It was Queen Elizabeth. She was crowned that day.

Anyway, it was a good coincidence really and cheered Dad up. He was a bit disheartened about having yet another daughter. He'd been *really* depressed four years before when my sister Sue was born. He was convinced she'd be a boy and organised a big party up at the farm for his fishing mates. Then 'George' turned out to be Sue and he was humiliated.

I think he was humiliated about the farm too. He'd bought it so that the family would be self-sufficient when the depression came. He had this theory that depressions follow wars. He'd thought it up in 1941 while he was in the navy, watching for underwater enemy activity.

He'd signed up the day war was declared and spent the next six years sitting on the Harbour Bridge waiting for the Japs to come. He waited and waited, but was on day leave the day they did. He was pretty bitter about it all, especially when it was all over. He'd tried to join the Returned Soldiers' League in 1945 but they wouldn't accept him because he hadn't returned from anywhere. Well, anywhere except the northern pylon.

2

So then he waited for a depression to come and of course it didn't. There was a boom instead. This meant the mountain place was empty most of the time with Dad working on his business. He never was able to use it to save his family from hunger and poverty. Mum said the post-war boom was one of his greatest disappointments.

Not that we were rich. We lived in Glebe in a house rented from the Church of England. The Church owned most of the houses in Richmond Street then. They were tiny semis or tenements filled with massive pieces of furniture. It was like that—the poorer you were, the bigger your wardrobe and dressing table had to be. Rich people from big houses used to give the things away and, if you were poor enough, you had to take them. If you were really poor you had to take lots of odd chairs too, and radiograms that didn't work any more. Sometimes the houses got so full of odd chairs and lowboys that there was hardly enough room for the children at all.

That's why so many people came out into the street after tea and stayed there until it was dark. It was pretty interesting. We lived right near the troting park and the greyhound track, so we got to watch the old men exercise the animals up and down every afternoon. The little men wore grey felt hats and held two or three dogs in one hand and a well-sucked Rothmans in the other. They gathered on the corner and talked about Blue Streak or Lord Charger while the dogs stood with their thin tails tucked hard along their sunken bellies and whined through muzzles. The local kids would play cricket on the road and the

3

husbands would smoke fags on the verandah and the mothers would stay inside and try to rearrange the chairs. Everybody knew everybody and watched who came and went and when they did.

Sue and I kept track from the window in the front room. We weren't allowed to run wild after tea. Maybe because we were girls or maybe because Dad was frightened that we'd disappear.

That happened a lot in our street. People disappearing. One day someone was there and the next day they weren't. Nobody talked about them after they'd gone.

I was only three or four when I first noticed it with Susan Parkes' father. The Parkes lived at the end of the street and probably had more odd chairs than anybody else. Susan was the youngest with about five brothers and sisters. You'd never know they were from the same family though because they all looked different. Her oldest sister was even part Aboriginal. One day Mr Parkes went to work and never came back. That's when Mrs Parkes put her head in the oven and disappeared as well. Then Susan stopped coming outside and we never saw her again either. The street sucked up lots of families like that, but particularly fathers and sons. Like Johnnie Herrington. He was always vanishing. He was about fifteen and had lots of tattoos. He'd come home with a new car or a wireless or lots of money in his pocket and within a few days some policemen would arrive and Johnnie would be gone again. Just when he was starting to do well, too.

And there were the people who disappeared because they were sick, especially the women. You could always tell who'd be the next to go. They'd get either very thin or very fat. The thin ones had TB and sometimes would never come back. The fat ones had babies and usually came back, but not always with the babies. Children got polio and came back with braces on their legs, and old people just lay down and died. There was a lot of coming and going and funerals and visiting the courts. That's where Mum's black net pillbox hat came in handy. All the ladies in the street borrowed it when they needed to dress up.

Mum was like a princess in Richmond Street. Everyone called her Mrs Sayer because she had the hat and Dad had a trade. He was a third-generation master painter. He'd take his ladder and brushes with him on the trams in the mornings and bring them home very afternoon. If there was no work he'd paint our place to keep in practice. From the outside it looked as bad as everyone else's, but inside it was all done up. The house got smaller and smaller with all those layers of Royal Magenta and Arctic Blue, but it was pretty exciting. You never knew what colour the kitchen was going to be next.

We had the phone on and were the first people to buy a television. The Herringtons got one not long after but it was the kind where you had to put a shilling in the meter every time you wanted to watch something. Ours worked for nothing because we were a bit better off. We didn't have much more money than everybody else, but at least Mum never had to wear the black pillbox herself.

The whole family, except for Dad, went to church every Sunday. It was the big Anglican one on the corner, the one that owned all the houses. Mum cut our dresses out on the kitchen table and ran them up on the Singer. They were all the same, except in different colours, which Rhonda hated because she was fifteen and I was only five and she felt ridiculous. We all wore gloves and hats and carried tiny purses with the plate money in them. We took three pennies each every week. One for the Sunday School, one for the missionaries and one for the Church. Sue always kept the Church penny for herself because she reckoned if it was rich enough to buy all those houses then it didn't need her money.

Sue, four years older than me, was the entrepreneur of the family, and a really good swimmer. Mr Hill, the swimming teacher at the pool, said she might be the next Dawn Fraser. Mum and Dad got worried about that because Dawn Fraser's shoulders were so big that she looked like a man. They stopped the lessons straight away. Sue was short and blond and took after Dad.

Rhonda was ten years older than me. She was the eldest, dark and slim, and looked a lot like Mum.

'Why have you got all that bloody muck on your face, Rhonda?'

'Because I'm going out, Dad.'

'No, you're not.'

'Why not?'

'Not with all that bloody muck on your face you're not.'

Dad and Rhonda had the same fight all the time.

6

She'd come down to tea with make-up all over her face and Dad would put his foot down. It was pretty frightening living with Rhonda because you never knew what she was going to look like next. Her bedroom walls were plastered with pictures of movie stars. She'd spend ages doing herself up like Annette Funicello or Doris Day and then sit around all night, legs crossed in her brunch coat, waiting to be allowed out. I got really scared when she was in her Beatnik phase with her face as white as a sheet and her eyes all black. She looked so sick that I thought she would disappear for sure. The fights with Dad would go on for ages with neither of them giving in. The worst was when she grew her thumb nail.

Rhonda was very particular about her appearance. She loved her nails especially and really looked after them. She wouldn't even play Scrabble because she reckoned you chipped your polish when you picked the letters up. Anyway, for some reason her thumb nail started to grow faster than all the others and she was obsessed with it. It made Dad sick to look at it, and he told her she had to cut it. She wouldn't, and it grew and grew. The whole family watched until it was almost long enough to butter bread with. That's when Dad blew up and Rhonda went mad and *bit* it off. Right there, in front of him. I think she must have frightened Dad by that because the next week he let her out with the boy next door, named Bob.

She had been seeing him secretly for months, anyway. No one knew except Sue. Rhonda would give Sue her old lipsticks so she'd carry the love letters back and forth. She got lolly money on delivery from Bob as well, and was very disappointed when Dad relented and Rhonda got to carry her own letters. Things settled down for Rhonda after that except for the odd flare-up like Mum hiding her bikini or letting out her pedalpushers or confiscating her eyebrow tweezers. Rhonda and Bob got serious pretty quickly and it wasn't long before he was in our place almost every night.

This created a new tension. Not that we didn't like him. We did. It was more to do with the telly. The arrival of television at our place in 1957 generated incredible changes. The lounge room became the TV room overnight and we had to buy a lot of new furniture. There were TV chairs and TV tables and even TV cups and saucers. But despite all these purchases there were never enough seats, and some of us had to take the pouf or sit on the floor.

We had a carefully worked-out system of rules. Whoever got a chair first could keep it for the whole night, so long as they said 'I bags this' if they needed to go to the toilet or answer the door or something. However, even with a 'bagsing' you lost your spot if you stayed away for more than two commercial breaks. The only person who was exempt from these rules was Dad, who could come and go when he liked, but I don't know why. Mum usually took the pouf voluntarily because she couldn't stand all the fighting.

When Bob started coming it threw the system right out. Good manners demanded that, as a visitor, he could have any chair (except Dad's) without any bagsing at all. On the other hand, he came so much that he wasn't really a visitor. In the end we accepted him into the family and he had to sit by the same rules as the rest of us. He never got used to it, though...he was always shocked when he'd get up and the girls would throw themselves into the seat screaming about 'bags'. He was particularly surprised when even Rhonda started doing it.

He never got used to Nana's noises, either. She broke wind constantly in front of the telly, in loud, long bursts, and all the girls knew we weren't allowed to laugh or say anything. We'd all sit there as though nothing was happening, surrounded by pops, blurps and bad smells, and Bob thought we were crazy. But every family has its own rituals, even in Glebe.

We had another one on Friday nights. We always ate fish. Not that we were Catholic, it was just a habit Mum got into during Lent one year. She gave up sugar in her tea the same way. Fish nights were always stressful because Mum and Dad were paranoid about one of the girls choking to death on a bone. Mum would watch us so carefully that if you so much as cleared your throat, you knew you were in for it.

'Jesus, Sid, she's got a bone in her throat.'

Dad'd be up quick as a flash and before you could say 'Jack Robertson' you'd be upside down being shaken by the ankles. The dog would be barking and going crazy and Dad would be screaming: 'Give us some bread, give us some bloody bread!'

Four or five slices of Tip Top would be shoved in your mouth and you knew you had to swallow the lot before the procedure would stop. It was a big price to pay for a nice piece of fried flathead, and the ritual went on for years. It only changed when we all got too heavy for Dad to lift and Mum started buying the fish fingers.

Rhonda said the fingers had no food value, which upset Mum because she was only trying to do the best thing by us. Rhonda was always coming out with these radical concepts that she learnt at the domestic science high school. She wouldn't do the wiping up, even when it was her turn, because she reckoned it spread disease. She said there were four and a quarter million germs in every square inch of tea towel, even clean ones. She was only trying to get out of work, though. As always. Rhonda was pretty slack really. You only had to take a good look at the state of her bra straps to see that she let a lot of germs and dirt pass unchecked.

Girls only went to the domestic science schools until they got the Intermediate Certificate. There was no provision for matriculation students at all. There were a lot of these schools in the 1950s. They were especially designed to turn young girls into good wives and that only took only three years. If you were smart enough to matriculate then you were probably unsuited to be a wife and shouldn't have been sent there in the first place. But dom science was good enough for Rhonda. She'd never even thought of going to the university. No one in Richmond Street did. She left school as soon as she could and went to business college. She was very conscientious and practised her shorthand in front of the telly every night. In the end she could get down almost every word of *BP Pick a Box*, except when Barry Jones was on. She said he talked too fast and it was too hard to hear. That's because the whole family was talking to the telly at the same time.

'Take the money, Barry.'

'No, no, the box...the box.'

'The money, the money.'

BP Pick a Box was our family's first real chance at a good education.

I'd just started school myself and kindie wasn't as challenging as TV, that's for sure. The teachers seemed to spend most of the day telling you either to sit down or look at your feet. We looked down a lot, mainly to check our shoes and socks. I was put into the top stream straight away and Mum was really proud of me. She didn't know that the assessment system was based purely on who could tie their shoelaces. Still, once you were placed that seemed to be it because the top class stayed much the same right through school.

I did pretty well and got to be toilet monitor. This was a very important position involving getting everyone to the toilet before there was an accident in the classroom. I had to keep my eye out because it took some kids a long time to realise they didn't have to wait until playtime if they couldn't hold on. It was pretty easy to tell. Suddenly a kid would sit up really straight and start wiggling his legs. You knew that if they scrunched up their faces there wasn't much time and if they started to cry, then you just got the mop out. Kerry Richards cried so often she was put into the bottom class, even though she was probably faster than anybody at tying her laces.

At the end of first year my work as toilet monitor

was rewarded. I was the star of the school play. The real star, the one that guides the Wise Men to the stables. Mum made me a huge cardboard star that was pinned to my back. It was so tall that the top point reached right over my head. She glued lots of metallic glitter all over it. The glitter was the problem. I stood on a chair at the side of the stage. When Mary took the baby Jesus out of the milk crate I was supposed to turn my head to the Three Wise Men and smile to guide them across the stage. But my hair got caught up in the glitter and glue and I just couldn't move it. The Three Wise Men were too stupid to realise what was happening and wouldn't come. In the end I had to get off my chair and pull them across and I was never made toilet monitor again.

Of course, the older we became the less important that job was anyway. Even Kerry Richards got the idea eventually.

In first class there was lots of reading and writing and learning how to cut up coloured pieces of paper. In second class there was sewing too. I never did well with that, though, because I was superstitious. 'See a pin and pick it up and all the day you'll have good luck.' There were so many pins wedged in the floorboards of the sewing room that I collected years of good fortune while the other kids just cross-stitched huck-a-back tray covers.

Our family was thick with superstitions. If you want to get married you should never drink out of a green straw, take the last biscuit from a plate or have two teaspoons on your saucer. There were so many things to remember, like not putting new shoes on the table. Mrs Wella did that with a new pair of sandshoes for her daughter Janice and the very next day Janice disappeared under the big wheels of a scrap-metal truck. The only thing left was one of the shoes, still white except for the tread of a back tyre. The street talked about that shoe for years and years. It was another of the rituals.

I was jealous of all the attention Janice got, even if she *was* dead. You feel like that when you're the youngest, particularly if you were an 'accident' like me. An 'accident' is like what Kerry Richards had or women had sometimes with their 'curse'. It's something that you weren't expecting and you don't want. And that was me.

My sisters mostly ignored me. Especially Rhonda. Sue let me play with her sometimes because she knew I'd be so grateful that I'd do anything. She'd let me ride down the hill on the back of her scooter, as long as I pushed her and the scooter all the way back up. And she got me to help her make money.

We stole the telephone box once. It was a Commonwealth Bank savings box that the neighbours put money in when they came to make phone calls. Sue waited until it was almost full and then got stuck into it with a tin opener. We bought new pencils and rubbers and Perkins paste and lots of lollies. We hid the chocolates in our pillow slips so we didn't have to eat them all at once. Mum found out when she tried to put four Scorched Peanut Bars and seven Cherry Ripes through the wringer on washing day and then Dad put us 'in gaol'. There was no pocket money or television for six weeks. We were put in gaol again when Sue sold all our clothes to the rag man for two and six. Dad was really furious because he reckoned they were worth a lot more than that. He was right, too, because the man charged him four shillings to get them back.

I think Sue was driven to steal because in our family there never seemed to be enough of anything. Never enough sample bags from the Easter Show, never enough crusts on a loaf of bread, never enough cream on the top of the milk and never enough games to play. We thought we'd cracked the shortage of games when we were given a hundred and one of them at Christmas. That's what it said on the box, anyway. It turned out to be a disappointment. There were really only Chinese Chequers and Snakes and Ladders and ninety-nine different sets of rules. Dad said it was a real con and Sue said it was pathetic. And I was left to play by myself.

It was hard finding a private spot because that's another thing families as big as ours can't get enough of. At first I tried playing in the toilet which was right down the back of the yard. Dad put a stop to it when Rhonda said I'd get hepatitus, so then I tried the dog kennel. This was even smaller than the toilet and got pretty crowded with my dolls and toys and the old dog too. But I liked it, and Sally, the dog, proved to be the best listener I'd ever had. Just when I was really settling in Rhonda said it wasn't hygenic and I could get the mange. She'd reckoned the old bird aviary was dangerous, too, because budgies carried polio. I knew this was ridiculous. When did you ever see a budgerigar in a leg brace? But Mum and Dad always did what Rhonda said in matters like this. She had all the weight of the domestic science certificate behind her. Just when I'd worked out there wasn't one safe place to play in the whole house, Dad announced we were going to move.

Business had been going well and he didn't need to take the ladder on the tram any more. He bought a Holden ute and had his name painted along the side. We used the truck for our get-away from Richmond Street.

The preparations were carried out in secret. Dad was really keen on getting his family away before the street sucked us up. He said if we didn't get out now, we never would. He must have felt bad about all the people who had to stay behind, though, because we weren't allowed to tell anyone until just before we went.

He sold the farm and borrowed money from his friend Merv. Merv was an SP bookmaker who had lots. He kept it in his pockets and when he went to the trots he closed them off from the inside with big safety pins to foil the pickpockets. He had to go to the toilet and take his trousers down whenever he wanted to make a bet. Some nights he pulled them down fifteen or twenty times and that's probably why some people called him 'Merv the perv'. He wasn't one, though, he was just cautious. Like Dad.

The day we left Richmond Street all the neighbours came out to see us off. Well, all except Mrs Williams. She was still in hospital after cracker night. Johnnie Herrington had put the cracker box too near the bonfire and a skyrocket went off and landed down her back. It was really terrible because it was a whistling one so no one heard her screaming for ages. We knew we were just getting out in time.

Mum left her black pillbox hat with Mrs Herrington and quite a few chairs with the other ladies and we drove off. Dad was saving his family from tragedy at last, or so he thought. He hadn't counted on Rhonda bringing the curse of Richmond Street with her.

We'd only been in the new house a few hours when she unpacked a whole suitcase of shoes right on to the kitchen table. We all remembered Janice and what a little pair of sandshoes could do, and here was Rhonda, with thongs and stilettos and almost new sling-backs. Mum pushed them on to the floor straight away, but it was too late. There would be tragedies in Bexley too.

2

The Tragedy

It was hard to imagine that things could go wrong.

It was 1960 and Bexley made us feel that anything was possible. It was a whole new world where houses had front yards and back yards and driveways running right along the side. Even if you didn't have a car you knew you had somewhere to put one if you ever did. Nothing could stand in your way. The houses were big and single-storey and never joined to each other. It was nothing like Glebe.

For a start, our place was incredible. We bought it on women's intuition. Mum said it smiled at her the first time she saw it. I don't think it was Mum in particular, though. It would probably have smiled at any normal Australian family after all the sadness with the Italians who were selling it.

Mr Rossellini did it up for his fiancée and then she went and married someone else. She wasn't Australian either—you could tell from the carpet. It was brand new with giant coloured flowers and spread right out to the skirting boards. It made you sick to look at it, but Dad wouldn't pull it up until it wore out and that took twelve years because Mr Rossellini hadn't skimped on quality. He'd obviously spent a lot on the chandeliers, too, because they lasted forever. We got used to them, though, except for the one in the kitchen. Mum made Dad replace that with a fluorescent light straight away. She said she could only take just so much.

The Henleys said the fluorescent was a good start in doing the house up. They were the people who lived next door. It took us eight months to meet them because in Bexley the houses were big enough for people to stay inside most of the time. Absolutely nobody ran wild after tea.

The Henleys lived on our right-hand side and were so refined that they didn't even have children. They had silver cutlery and furniture with spindly legs and crystal glasses in the sideboard. We had some crystal, too, but we weren't well off enough to *use* ours. The Henleys drank sherry every night before tea and ate in the dining room. They had a big old cat called Arthur. Well-off people generally prefer cats to dogs, though I don't know why. They give them human names, too, like Henry or Cynthia, while poor people choose Spot or Mutt or Fluffball. I think if Johnnie Herrington's parents had given him the sort of care Arthur got from the Henleys, Johnnie wouldn't have disappeared half as much. Bexley was so different. Mr Henley was the first man I'd ever met who mowed the lawn with his shirt on and watched the ABC voluntarily. In Glebe nobody watched it, and I'm not even sure the antennae could pick it up.

The Henleys said they were really pleased that we'd taken over the house from Rossellini, the New Australian. They didn't call him wog or dago or anything, but you could tell they preferred an Old Australian family, even one from Glebe. Mr Henley had been down on migrants ever since he'd found a Greek family from Arncliff having a picnic on his front lawn. The Henleys' garden had lots of trees and special grass with no bindis that was as smooth as a bowling green, so I guess the Greeks thought it was a park. Mr Henley might have let them stay, too, if only they hadn't parked their Holdens in the driveway and put the barbecue right under his Christmas bush. It was the closest thing to a People's Revolution that Bexley had ever seen. The story worried Dad and made Mum wonder if she really should have left her black pillbox in Glebe after all. It was the first inkling that tragedy might find us in Bexley after all. But I could understand that this was different. I loved the Henleys' front lawn just as much as the Greeks. It made you feel better than you thought you really were.

And sometimes that was a comfort, especially on Saturday afternoons when the Frangipani Lounge was having a function. The Frangipani was a reception house, two doors down, on the other side of the Henleys. It was beautiful with tall columns on the verandah and a circular driveway so that the bride could be delivered right to the door. It was a lot like a stately home in England. Just smaller and in Bexley. And there were so many trees you could hardly hear the traffic noise at all. It was a fairyland. The owners lived in a garage down the back.

Every Saturday afternoon Rhonda and Sue would interrupt their beauty treatments to crouch amongst the Henleys' ferns and take a squizz at the wedding parties. They wouldn't just stand out the front with me and Mum and the other ladies because they felt ridiculous with their hair in rollers and their brunch coats on. They looked more ridiculous half-hidden amongst the fishbone and the maidenhair, though. Like two garden gnomes getting ready for a big night out. Rhonda and Sue never a missed a wedding. They were doing their research for Rhonda's own marriage to Bob later on in the year. It would be the biggest day of her life and the time of our family's first major tragedy.

In the meantime I was having trouble settling in at school. It was an all-girl primary with the boys in a separate building across the road. It was certainly a lot safer like that with no one pushing your face into bubblers or knocking you flat when you stood in the milk line, but it took a bit of getting used to. In Glebe, you could get whatever you wanted from the boys just by letting them like you. At the new school, no one liked me for quite a while.

There was no doubt about it, I got off to a bad start. The third class teacher was an old woman called Miss Maffer. She was very fat and had dry rough hands with chalk dust embedded in the cracks. On my first day I ran into the children's toilet and found her propped on one of the tiny bowls with her big white cotton panties rolled down around her ankles. Her bottom was so big it spread right over the seat and flapped down near the gound as well. She looked horrible, but sounded even worse. She started off with huffs and puffs and then it came, like a waterfall, on and on. I thought she must have some problem in the waterworks for sure.

In class that afternoon she suddenly sat up very straight at her table and started wriggling her legs. My year as toilet monitor in Glebe was not in vain. I raced out of my seat and said I'd take her to the toilet. Now! That's when her face scrunched up so I said, from my experience, she didn't have much time. I asked her where she kept the mop, just in case.

She shouted and screamed and hit me across the back of my legs with a ruler. She said people in Bexley 'had no trouble hanging on, thank you very much'. She wrote a letter to give to Mum. The other girls laughed so much that two of them made little puddles under their desks and the mop came out after all. I wasn't allowed to get it, though. They already had a monitor, Gillian Gallagher, and from what I could see she did a pretty good job.

Everyone had a special duty and everyone had a special friend. They were mostly very clean girls from good homes. In Glebe, my tin of twelve Cumberland coloured pencils with the lake picture on the front was always hotly in demand and I made as many friends as I liked. In Bexley, the Cumberlands were hardly worth borrowing. Everyone had them. Some girls even had the full set of seventy-two Derwents.

Access to a box of Derwents meant top marks in your projects every time. A subtlety of colour and tone was possible in your headings and you could make rivers and mountains look really beautiful. The girls with the Derwents were very confident and ruled the roost. They became class captain and were usually the only child in their family.

I would have killed to be an only child. As far as I could see they were the closest thing Australia had to English princesses. They got little surprises in their lunch boxes and pressed hankies in their pockets and mothers who waited at the gate to walk them home. They had piano lessons and ballet classes and went to Queensland on their holidays. Only children had so many advantages—like a family block of chocolate that only had to be shared three ways.

By the end of third class I had one best friend, Sandra Coutts. The good part: she was an only child, had the complete Derwents and could never eat all her lunch. The bad part: she disappeared. I knew it was coming. She was an asthmatic and actually that was the only way she got to be my friend at all. The other girls wouldn't sit next to her because they were scared. It was all the wheezing, I think. The room would be very quiet and then Sandra's chest would begin to rumble and she'd gasp for breath and the other girls would start to cry. It didn't frighten me because I'd seen people disappear before. Anyway, we'd only been friends for a few months when she stopped coming to school and then she just died. I cried for quite a while, but even now I don't know whether it was for Sandra or the Derwents. I think it was probably the pencils, though, because for months afterwards I daydreamed about her parents finding a will hidden in her bedroom. It said all seventy-two Derwents were for me. It also asked her mother to make me a special lunch box every day for a year. She never did.

Mum tried hard, but she never had the gift for packaging food. For example, she always put tomato in the sandwiches which made them soggy. This was the sort of thing Mrs Coutts would never do. Not that Mum wasn't a good cook. She was. She made tripe and brains and kidneys on toast and special lamb's fry and spaghetti. Our family was pretty adventurous about food, mainly through my father. He was always willing to try anything. That's how he came to have no teeth. When he was little he found a bottle of lemonade and drank it. It turned out to be poison and burnt up all the teeth in his head. Right down to small stumps. So he had false ones, like a lot of people then. Nana did too.

This made meal times very noisy with Dad and Nana sucking their gums and twirling their tongues under their teeth in search of stray bits of food. It was important to find all the crumbs because they rubbed and made ulcers if left too long. Chopped nuts were particularly tricky. It was a pretty ugly process, especially with Nana. She'd had enough ulcers in her life to teach her to do a really thorough search. She sucked and twirled her way right through tea, and then she'd pop her plates out altogether and rinse them in the sink before dessert. Just to make sure.

If she did get an ulcer she wouldn't wear her teeth

for days and that was even worse. She was a happy cockney woman who talked all the time, even when she had a mouth full of gums, white tea and soggy Milk Arrowroots. Whenever she laughed spit balls of biscuit would fly out in all directions and land in your milk, or in Dad's beer or on to Rhonda's new brunch coat. We weren't allowed to say anything about it, either. Mum and Dad were really strict about that and we had to fish out the biscuit without Nana seeing. I don't think it would have embarrassed her, though. She'd always been so poor that no teeth and flying food were a normal part of life. And it was funny, but in Glebe it hadn't annoyed us so much. There was something about Bexley that made you want to do things nicely. It inspired you to try just that bit harder.

Maybe that's why Mum decided to learn to drive. Dad was dead set against it, and even when she finally got her licence he wouldn't let her drive further than around the block for a whole year. This was mainly because we lived on a busy road surrounded by dangerous intersections. On Sundays, Dad would back the truck out of the drive and then Mum would take over and we'd drive around the block for hours at a time. She'd practise her reverse parks and three-point turns and sometimes would defy Dad and drive further on where the road was steep so she could do her hill starts. She got very frustrated having to stay within Dad's limits and finally he let her take small trips, like to visit her sister, Aunty Lou. Aunty Lou only lived in the next suburb but sometimes it would take Mum three or four hours to get there. Every week she'd get out her Gregory's and we'd drive to Lou's via Wollongong or Parramatta and keep the details of the route a secret.

I always went with Mum on these drives because no one else would and I felt sorry for her. Also, the dangerous intersections surrounding our house stopped me from getting about much on my own anyway. For a long time Dad wouldn't let me cross them, either.

This made things hard because all the girls from school lived on the other side of the road. I spent a lot of time walking around and around the block, watching them playing just two car-widths away. Sometimes I walked it backwards or blindfolded or by pogo stick which made things a little more interesting but it was still pretty lonely.

And Sally the dog was getting too old to be much company either. For a start, she wasn't allowed inside because of her bad smells. She got away with them for a long time because we thought they were coming from Nana. I don't know who Nana thought they were coming from.

Anyway, one night Nana wasn't there and the smells were worse than ever so Mum banned Sally from then on. Rhonda and Sue were pretty happy about it; they'd been campaigning to get rid of Sally for ages. They said she looked disgusting, sort of mental. It was her tongue. It hung out the side of her mouth because there weren't enough teeth left to hold it in. Nana and Sally had a lot in common actually, and if Rhonda and Sue had got their way Nana probably wouldn't have been let in either. But

Mum made these decisions and so Nana stayed. Once we had settled in Bexley, Mum's power in the family began to grow. Especially after she got her own car, a Morris Minor. We pretended Dad was still important, of course, but in real 'getting what you want' terms, Mum had the final say.

'Mum, can I . . . ?'

'You'll have to ask your father.'

'Dad, can I . . . ?'

'As long as it's all right with your mother.'

I think Dad was just a victim of the changing times. Australia was really moving ahead fast and Bexley was at the vanguard of those changes. Dad saved us from the street of the disappearing people only to start disappearing himself. It's strange the way things happen. He worked harder and made more money and the business went from strength to strength. And he got more tired and his heart started to play up and Mum grew more and more powerful.

Once she got the keys to the Morris there was no holding her back. She joined the golf club and the hospital auxiliary and drove from one end of Sydney to the other. Every new appliance was another nail in the coffin of Dad's supremacy. The Simpson automatic allowed Mum to do an entire family wash and play nine holes of golf at the same time. The Hoover with the nozzle attachments could beat as it swept as it cleaned. The house buzzed with electrical energy and some of this must have transferred to Mum and maybe us girls too. Dad hardly got a word in over tea any more, and soon he was bagsing his spot in front of the telly, just like the rest of us.

28

Not that he liked television all that much. He only watched the Westerns. I think the other programmes probably embarrassed him. You know, all the family shows from America, like *Father Knows Best* and *Leave It to Beaver* and *Bachelor Father*. There was such a big difference between the sort of father Dad was and the sort they had in these shows. Not that he wasn't a good man. He was. It's just that he didn't talk to us much or call me Princess or Honey or anything like that. He never cuddled or kissed us, either. I mean, I can understand that. He was a man's man and that was that.

That didn't stop us from trying to change him. We'd seen enough American families jumping into wood-panelled station wagons for a day at the lake to know that things at our place could be better. Mum started organising picnics, but they weren't a great success. For a start, we all couldn't fit in the Morris. Dad was a wake-up straight away and used the little Morris as an excuse to go fishing with his mates instead. Then Sue was inspired by an episode of *My Three Sons* and suggested things the family could do at home, like a weenie roast and a marshmallow melt. The roast was a failure because no one knew what a weenie was, and the melt fizzled out when one marshmallow dropped off the skewer and blew up the new heater, the Vulcan Conray Delux.

I began calling Dad different names. I tried Father, Daddy and Hey, Pop. He hated them all. Then I tried sitting on his knee, but he got so embarrassed he started crossing his legs, like Rhonda did, whenever he sat down. Acutally, I feel pretty guilty about that now—crossed legs are bad for your heart. And, as it turns out, Dad's heart was his big problem.

Dad was just an ordinary bloke who called a bob a bob, and then, through no fault of his own, a bob became ten cents. A quid became two dollars, and Australia became part of the real world. Once television showed us what life could be like it was hard to be satisfied with what you had. And it wasn't just the telly, either.

I started to read a lot and found I could pretend to be other people. I could be anyone I liked and that made life seem much more exciting than it really was. Now I think about it, if Mum had been more like Donna Reed and Dad more like *Bachelor Father* and if I'd been someone's 'kid sister', instead of 'the little brat', then maybe I wouldn't have wanted to read so much. And then I would never have got my first job at school.

Mrs Skillicorn picked me to be library monitor because I borrowed more books than anybody else. I read everything but I particularly liked the English stories about the girls who went away to school and had midnight feasts with crumpets. Reading helped to dispel a lot of my fears, which was good for me, but not so good for Dad.

'One more word out of you, Moya, and you'll be off to boarding school: no bloody risk about that.'

'Can it be Miss Everleigh's in Sussex, Dad? Or Miss Princey's in Durham?'

He wasn't too keen on my efforts to improve my vocabulary, either.

'Where's the sugar, Moya?'

'On the bureau, Dad.'

'On the what?'

'Oh, on the sideboard.'

'Well, why don't you say the bloody sideboard?'

Because Anne of Green Gables says 'bureau'.

The Secret Seven said 'bureau' too. They were this group of kids in England who got together to solve crimes. For a while I tried to live like them. I formed the Secret One and spent a lot of time at the bus stop making notes on the people who got off the 327. I soon found out that Bexley must be pretty tame compared to Buckinghamshire because there was hardly a suspicious character to be found. I exaggerated a little, I guess.

'5:15 p.m. Bus 327. Man in black overcoat, grey hat. Six foot six approx. Distinguishing feaures: Scar on right cheek, bad limp, three fingers on left hand. Russian accent.'

As soon as I had a whole exercise-book filled with suspects I showed it to Sue. I wanted her to join my society, partly because it gets pretty lonely spending every afternoon at the bus stop by yourself, but mainly because the Secret Two sounds a lot better than the Secret One. Sue just looked at the book and said I was pathetic. She said I'd made it all up. She said it was so obvious: 'The last 327 leaves at 4 p.m. for a start.'

Sue knew all the timetables. She spent most afternoons riding the buses so she couid meet the boys. They were the same boys she saw at high school every day, but apparently they only became interesting after 3:15. Sue no longer found me interesting no matter what time it was, I just annoyed her. This was very disturbing because she'd always been my idol. Once she turned thirteen it didn't take much to get on her nerves. If I laughed at something on the telly, she'd hiss through her teeth and leave the room. Suddenly, she hated the way I walked, talked, ate, everything. Even the sound of my breathing. It got so bad, with Rhonda joining in, that I practised taking quiet, shallow breaths and smiling with my mouth shut to keep the laughs in.

By the time we found out about Rhonda's tragedy my breathing was so shallow that I knew I could get a job in the movies for sure. You know, as one of the dead people. I always watched those dead bodies very carefully to work out how they kept their chests so still. Maybe they had a sister like Sue too. Anyway, once the tragedy happened no one had time to care how I was breathing, or even if I was. As Mum said, 'It came as such a shock.'

The plans for Rhonda's wedding had been going ahead for almost a year. Sue would be bridesmaid. Every Tuesday night the girls went out with Mum in the Morris to visit the dressmaker. There was so much to get made with the bridal gowns and Rhonda's going-away ensemble and Mum's shantung frock. Rhonda's dress was finished first so Mum had time to sew hundreds of little pearls on the train. She did it every night in front of the telly. It was the only time that Mum had first say to the Jason recliner.

Rhonda's trousseau was already pretty well in hand. She'd been laybying petticoats and nighties for her glory box ever since she started work. Her box was a big old wardrobe with deep drawers that reaked of naphthalene. It had things for the house as well, like cups and saucers and crystal vases and silver cake trowels. A lot of the best stuff, like the silver-plated cake tray, was engraved in the centre with 'Best Lady All Rounder' or 'Winner 36 Handicap' because they were Mum's golf trophies that she didn't want. Rhonda didn't mind about the writing. She reckoned you could get away with it as long as you always kept one piece of cake in the middle. But even Rhonda didn't know what to do with putter-shaped fondue forks and the tea towels printed with 'Golf Courses of the World'.

I used to spend a lot of time going through Rhonda's box, just taking things out and putting them back in again. That's how I found *The Book for Brides*. The most interesting chapter was called 'Your First Night'. The author advised that it be spent in a hotel not too far from the reception house. She said the bride should pack a few essentials like sanitary napkins, a small hand towel and an alarm clock. The clock was to wake up the newly-weds in the middle of the night...

Brides should remember that the wedding day will be very exhausting. Not just for you but for the groom as well. Young couples should shower and then go straight to sleep. Set the alarm clock for two or three hours and then awake, to begin your married life refreshed and relaxed...

The hand towel was to protect the bride from pain.

33

> Many new brides will be surprised by the size of their husbands' personal part. If it is so great as to cause pain, ask your husband to wrap the towel around the base of his member to reduce its length. Brides should not be embarrassed about asking this of their husbands. He wants you to enjoy your married life as much as he does.

They never explained what the sanitary napkins were for. Actually, as it turned out, Rhonda didn't even need to know. Her first night wasn't going to be her first at all. Rhonda was in trouble.

Not Rhonda. Not Rhonda. Pregnant. Not Rhonda. Mum and Dad couldn't believe it. They didn't know what to say. They tried.

Mum said, 'You're not a bad girl. Remember, only the nice girls get caught.'

Dad said, 'Nature just beat the wedding, that's all.'

It beat the kitchen tea, too. 'That was when Mum first realised that tragedy had struck.

The bridal shower had been going really well. We'd already had the games. We had Pass the Parcel, Memorise the Things on the Tray and Chinese Whispers. Then Rhonda opened the presents. There were lots of Tupperware and good-quality utensils and then, just as Rhonda was clucking over a lettuce crisper, her girlfriends from the office gave her a special parcel. It was a pair of baby bootees and a plastic rattle. It was a joke, of course, but Rhonda didn't know that. She just burst into tears and ran into the bedroom. Everyone put it down to nerves. Well, everyone but Mum.

The revelation threw the family into panic. As

34

Rhonda blossomed and thickened around the waist, the rest of the family began to shrink. It was all the tension, I think. Mum and Dad and Sue started to disappear before our eyes and then, on the big day, they just collapsed.

The morning started off well enough. It was a beautiful day and that cheered everyone up... 'The bride that the sun shines upon...' The girls got off to the hairdressers first thing and Dad went to the hire place in Hurstville to pick up his suit. Then the make-up girl came and did everyone's faces and the photographer arrived. He squeezed himself on to the lounge to wait between all the Corning ware and the parfait glasses and the salad bowls wrapped and tied in silver. He had to wait a long time because in the bedrooms things had ground to a halt. It started with Mum.

She slipped on her new frock and it almost slipped off her again. Then she saw Dad in his suit that looked two sizes too big. The shock was too much and sent them straight back to bed. In the other room, Sue saw that she was disappearing too. She was in tears stuffing handkerchiefs into her bra to replace the lost bosom. This was particularly upsetting because she hardly had any bosom to begin with. Of course, Rhonda's 'condition' meant she didn't need handkerchiefs, but she certainly needed her girdle. And she couldn't pull it on. Her nails were still wet, so she needed help and there was no one to give it to her. She sat on the bed and froze up.

Lucky for us Mr Newley arrived. He was the florist and he'd been doing weddings for forty years.

He reckoned he'd seen the lot and as soon as I told him what was going on he snapped into action. He got Mum and Dad out of bed, got the cotton balls out of the bathroom for Sue's bosom and then he went to work on Rhonda.

He reckoned she was almost catatonic. He stood her up, took off her brunch coat and got her to lean from the waist. He found her bra, slipped her arms through the straps and fastened the hooks at the back. By the time he'd pulled her girdle on she was more herself again. The family was assembled in the lounge room in ten minutes flat. Incredible. Then the photographer started making trouble.

It wasn't his fault, he just couldn't find a good wall for the backdrop. He was right. Mr Rossellini's wallpapering had been thorough and there wasn't a plain white wall left in the house. The lounge was flock Regency, the kitchen a Caribbean cabana, and the TV room a Swiss sauna. The photographer said the bride would just disappear into the patterns. This was the last straw for Dad. He reckoned there was enough disappearing going on already and he wouldn't stand for any more. He managed to save his family one more time. He flung a new painter's drop sheet over Mum's Morris in the driveway and the photos were taken just in time. It was a pity no one noticed Sally's food bowl, buzzing with flies, sitting just near Rhonda's feet.

The reception was held in the Tropicana Room, not the Frangipani Lounge as you might have thought. This was because of the brandy crustas. Brandy crustas are cocktails with sugar stuck to the edge of the glass. The Tropicana gave a free one to all the ladies with their hors-d'oeuvres. They gave you prawn cocktails for entrées, too, whereas the Frangipani served only fruit compote. The Tropicana threw in the services of an MC for nothing and had quite a cheap combo available for the dancing. Dad said it was too good to pass up.

You knew how important you were by how much of the bridal table you could see. I got stuck behind the water fountain with Nana, our aunty Jean with the big flashy breasts, and Johnnie Herrington's mother who was wearing Mum's old black pillbox. Mr and Mrs Henley and Mum's friends from the golf club were right up the front and were able to see everything. They got their food first, too, while it was still hot, and they probably managed to hear all the speeches. We couldn't hear anything. Not even the telegrams, and I was sorry about that. Bob's best man made up a lot of funny ones up because the real ones weren't funny at all.

Time just flew. Before you knew it we were running downstairs to see the newly-weds off. There was toilet paper hanging from Bob's FJ Holden and shaving cream signs on the window. There weren't any cans strung from the back, though. The MC wouldn't allow it because the Tropicana was right in the middle of a residential area and there'd been complaints. It didn't matter, there was enough noise anyway. There was whistling and shouting and the girls from Rhonda's office were sobbing and Mum and Mrs Herrington were crying and the biggest day in Rhonda's life was over. And then they were gone. Just like that.

They came back to the house the next day to pick

up their bags. And then after the honeymoon they moved into Rhonda's old room to save money. And then the photos came back. They were pretty disappointing, especially the ones taken in front of the Morris. For a start, the photographer had made Rhonda stand with one foot pointed in front of her which gave a nice line to her dress but really make the dog bowl look obvious. Mum and Dad were swimming in their clothes as if they'd borrowed them from somewhere, I looked ridiculous smiling with my mouth shut and in every photo of Sue there was a tiny piece of white peeking from her neckline. Mr Newley's cotton balls.

Mum wouldn't have shown the photos to people anyway. They brought the whole day back and made it feel as if it had just happened yesterday. And with Rhonda growing bigger everyday, yesterday wasn't early enough. Baby Linda arrived before the glue was dry in the albums. Poor Dad, another girl. She weighed in at an enormous ten and a half pounds. Poor Mum, she'd told all the ladies at the golf club that Linda was premature!

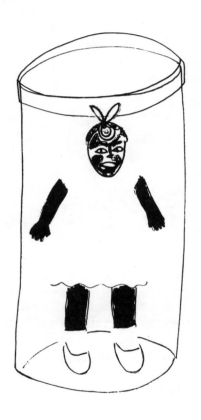

3

Neat Girls

There were now seven people living at home and the added numbers put a big strain on facilities. We had to buy a big double bed for Rhonda and Bob, a new extendable table for the kitchen, two new poufs for the television room and the bagsing system was applied to just about everything. Especially the bathroom. The bathroom was in constant use and contained the only toilet in the house.

'I bags the toilet after Rhonda.'

'No, your father's after Rhonda, then there's Sue.'

'Well, I bags the toilet after Rhonda, after Dad and after Sue.'

We spent a lot of time hopping around the little foyer waiting to get in. Sometimes the line was so long that we went back to catch a bit of telly to take our minds off it. It was torture for an ex-toilet monitor. The whole family would be wriggling their toes and scrunching their faces for hours on end.

'Sue, your father's busting. What are you doing in there?'

It was a mystery. What could you do in a bathroom that would take so long?

Then, through sheer accident, I discovered the nail brush. I was just lying in the bath one night checking the floatability of the flannel and the soap and other odds and ends when the nail scrubber popped up from its submarine base next to the shampoo bottle and rubbed between my legs. So that was it. It was terrific. I tried it again just to make sure. Incredible. I used the little brush every night after that and the queues for the bath became longer and longer. Mum had to start a booking system when Sue bought the new Swedish-pine back-scrubber and it was just as well. That scrubber was such bliss that the girls stayed underwater for hours, finally emerging like soft pink prunes. Without the booking system, the men would never have got into the bathroom at all.

I suppose the delays could have been shorter if we were the sort of family that allowed more than one person to use facilities at the same time. But we weren't. The bathroom was something private. No one got to see anybody's personal parts. Not even Mum and Dad. Well, not until Rhonda and Bob got married. For some reason they were allowed to go into the bathroom together and stay almost as long as they liked. They closed their door at night when they went to bed too. This was a bit of a shock. It had never happened before. Not with Mum and Dad. They always kept their door open and you knew what was happening. But Rhonda and Bob even shut their door during the day which made everybody embarrassed. The family tried to go on as usual, but it was very uncomfortable. It was the first time in our history that even a bagsing couldn't guarantee your inclusion.

With so many people it was almost impossible to get any attention paid to you through conventional methods. I had long given up on the idea that Sue would ever like me again. It was pretty clear that silent breathing and closed mouth smiling weren't getting me anywhere. With anyone. The only way to get any attention was to fight for it.

As the youngest I had a bit of an advantage through the 'cuteness factor'. I discovered that you could get people to listen to you by pretending that you weren't as smart as you really were. Like in front of the telly. Every Sunday night was movie night. At 8:30 p.m. the lounge would be jam-packed for the American movie. The film credits gave you an idea of whether the show was going to be any good. The cast names would begin to roll and the family would buzz with excitement.

'Come on, Sid, Ronald Reagan's in this.'

'Oooh, Deanna Durbin. I like her.'

'You beauty. John Wayne.'

I'd wait for my moment and then, when an obscure name came up beside Key Grip or Lighting Assistant, I'd cry out, 'Ooooh look, Joe Wilkins. I like him. This is going to be good!'

The family would roll with mirth.

'God, you're stupid!'

'Hear that, Sid? Joe Wilkins!'

'He's not in it, idiothead.'

43

It never failed to get a laugh. At other times it was sheer volume or persistence that won out. Especially over dinner. The idea was that if someone was talking when you wanted to talk, then you just talked louder. If you kept it up long enough then the other person would usually die away and then you had control. Until someone wanted it from you, of course. The decibel level was deafening but no one cared. Well, no one except Bob. He never seemed to get the hang of it and was the easiest person of all to talk out. Occasionally, Rhonda took over to help him along and then, when she'd won, she'd let him pick up his story again. Once they were married they were a hard team to beat. They were becoming a little family with rituals all their own.

But even Rhonda and Bob were no match for the new runway. They built it down at the airport and our house was right under the flight path. Mum reckoned the jets used her Hills Hoist to get their bearings and maybe they did. You could lie in the backyard and read the numbers on their silver bellies. They came that low.

The family must have got used to it. You'd hear the planes rumbling in the distance and at a certain moment everyone would stop talking. Just like that. It wasn't too bad. It gave you a bit of a rest to think about other things before the shouting started all over again. It was annoying when the telly was on, though. They always seemed to fly over in the best bits.

'Take the money, Barry.'

'No, the box.'

'No, the money, the money.'

VRRROOOOMMMM.

'What'd he say? What'd he bloody say?'

The new container trucks were a problem, too. They crashed and rumbled right past our door delivering TVs and furniture and building supplies to the new suburbs springing up down south. So with the planes and the trucks and all the fighting going on between the girls, there wasn't a quiet spot left in the house. It was a relief to go to school.

The survival techniques I was learning at home stood me in good stead for the classroom. My reports said I was 'boisterous and precocious and could do better', and soon I had so many friends I could start dropping some of the less colourful ones. I still couldn't make it into the 'only-child-full-set-of-Derwents' group, though. Those neat little girls always stuck together and whispered in tiny clusters. Their parents sent notes so they never had to do anything they didn't want to. The government made the rest of us drink warm milk at playtime while the neat girls drank icy orange juice from plastic thermoses. While we jumped around doing reels in the folk dancing every Friday morning, the neat girls sat under the trees colouring in their project headings. These girls knew they were special. Their leader was Jenny Sealey.

Jenny was an ugly girl with white freckled skin and pigtails tied in satin ribbons. She wore school shoes with chiselled toes and handmade jumpers with a pattern knitted into them. She was class captain and got top marks in most subjects. But she wasn't that

45

smart, she just had certain advantages. Like the full set of Derwents and a complete edition of the Encyclopaedia Britannica. Her father worked in a bank in the city and so she always got the best pictures for her projects.

For example, if we were doing an assignment on the great northern rivers, her father would go into the Queensland Tourist Bureau during his lunch hour and pretend he was planning a holiday. He'd get pamphlets with really good coloured photos and extra information. Girls like me who wrote letters would be sent the Student's Pack with only one or two pictures, usually in black and white. Dad would never get brochures for me. For a start, he never had a painting job in town and, secondly, he just couldn't be bothered. Mum and Dad were worn out as parents by the time they got to me. It was a no-nonsense approach to child-rearing, sink or swim. I usually sunk, but it wasn't for lack of trying.

Like Show and Tell. Once a week our fifth class teacher, Mrs Hanrahan, gave us an opportunity to bring new things into the classroom and talk about them. Mrs Hanrahan was pretty interesting herself. She was right into geography and she named her three daughters Victoria, Adelaide and Brisbane.

Anyway, I used to try very hard to get the vote for the most interesting possession. One time I took in Mum's new automatic putter. She used it to practise her golf in front of the telly at night. It was a little disc with a hole in the centre and a spring. If Mum got the ball in the hole then the spring would pop the ball back out again. Like a prize. Another time I took in Rhonda's false eyelashes.

I won the vote for the putter and I would have won it for the eyelashes, if it hadn't been for Jenny Sealey. Her uncle was an airline pilot and he gave her presents from all over the world. Usually they were dolls in national costume but the week I took in Rhonda's lashes he'd been to America and brought her back a laughing bag. This was a little machine like a tape recorder that played a really loud laugh over and over. The bag was a big hit, of course, with everyone laughing along and Jenny won the vote. She didn't say, 'I think your eyelashes should have won, Moya', or anything like that. She just lapped up all the attention. Jenny was really proud that she'd made the class laugh. It was probably the only time in her life she ever did.

If Rhonda's eyelashes had got the credit they deserved I wouldn't have lost my job as library monitor. Mrs Skillicorn, the librarian, organised a special doll show for Education Week. We were allowed to enter one each. It was hard for me to pick between Maryanne and Topsy Amanda. Maryanne was far and away my favourite, but she had different-coloured eyes. One blue and one brown. That was because they only had brown ones left at the doll hospital when we had put her in the year before. Mum said we should wait until they got more blue, but I didn't want Maryanne to wear a patch so that was that. A lot of girls at school wore patches then. They had pieces of brown paper stuck over one side of their glasses and they looked a bit mental. Maryanne deserved better than that.

Still, I knew that for the competition the odd eyes would go against her in the end so I decided to enter

Topsy Amanda. Topsy was black. She had fuzzy hair that was really short and shiny dark skin with red on her cheeks. Mum made her a special dress with big purple flowers and a headscarf with a curtain ring in the front. I thought Topsy would win for sure. I hadn't accounted for Jenny Sealey's uncle and Esmerelda.

He bought Esmerelda from Spain. She was a walking, talking bride doll and two and a half feet tall. Incredible. Her eyes could open and shut and if you fed her water she did little wees. I thought the weeing was unnecessary for a bride but the other kids obviously didn't agree. It was clear Esmerelda would get the votes.

It was a token system. Everyone paid two cents at the door and got a ticket to put in front of their favourite doll. As library monitor I gave them out. By the end of lunchtime it was looking bad for Topsy. Esmerelda had a big pile of votes and Topsy didn't have one. Not even my own. I'd given it to my best friend Rosalie to place for me and she'd been so overcome by Esmerelda's capabilities that she'd put my vote there too. There was only one thing to do and I did it.

In a quiet moment I grabbed a handful of unused tickets and stuck the lot in front of Topsy. Then, just to make up for the eyelashes, I took some more from Esmerelda's own pile. Topsy was the first black doll to win in the history of the competition. I got a family block of chocolate and a certificate. The next day Mrs Skillicorn confiscated the certificate and would have taken the chocolate too if the family hadn't already eaten it. A quick count of the votes had revealed that 800 people had visited the show. As there were only 300 girls in the whole school Topsy was in disgrace, Jenny Sealey got the certificate and I lost my job as monitor. Jenny was queen again, but not for long. She got undone by the Argentine ants.

At that time, Argentine ants were big news. They were tiny red insects that ate through wood and threatened to undermine the future of the Australian building industry. The industry was really starting to jump ahead with new housing developments springing up all over the suburbs. The Argentine ants were a public menace and the government called on schoolchildren throughout the nation to help.

This procedure had already been a huge success during the recent drought. The government had sent out special project packs full of pictures of bony cows gathered around dry river beds and skinny sheep about to drop dead. So many girls cried that Mrs Hanrahan took away the photos and gave us the stickers and badges instead. We were Australia's water wardens and our job was to watch out for leaky taps and people who violated the restrictions. You could report adults to the police if they left their sprinklers on or showered for more than five minutes. Some kids got so excited that they started reporting their own parents. Jenny Sealey did. She got another certificate, her parents were fined and Dad said it was just like bloody Hitler all over again.

Then there was the ant campaign. The idea was to find the Argentine, put it in a bottle marked with the place of discovery and then collect your certificate and reward money. Jenny was the only kid at school to lodge an entry. There was going to be a special assembly where she could give a speech and a man from the Hurstville Builders and Labourers Association would present the award. He never came. It turned out that Kerry's red ant wasn't Argentine at all. It was just an ordinary brown Australian one that she'd dyed red with the cochineal left over from toffee day. The trouble was it ended up a sickly lolly-pink colour instead. Jenny was thrown out of the inner circle in disgrace and that left a space on the far outer edge of it for me. I wanted to be a neat girl, too.

Mrs Coombes gave piano lessons in her lounge room in Dunsmore Street. I found her name on the notice-board at the municipal library.

MRS ELLEN COOMBES
TEACHER OF PIANO FORTE

I didn't know what sort of piano a forte was but Mum said I should ring anyway and ask if she also taught Palings Pianola. That's what we had in the living room—a big, black pianola. Rhonda and Sue had learnt on it when they were little, but as neither had lasted more than a few months I was faced with a history of family failure before I'd even begun. Once again my parents' efforts had been exhausted on the other girls and by the time it came to me no one cared one way or the other. I just had to arrange it. Maybe if Mum had met Mrs Coombes herself she would have found me another lady from the start.

Mrs Coombes was a lot like my third class teacher, Miss Maffer, the one with the chalk dust on her fingers. Mrs Coombes didn't have chalk dust, though, she had saliva. She sucked her fingers constantly while I played. She was a big woman with heaving breasts and legs so fat she couldn't rub her knees together. She sat almost on top of me with her legs splayed apart and smelt spicy and old like the drawers in Rhonda's glory box. And she spat.

She didn't mean to. There was just so much dribble gathered in her mouth with all the sucking that when she spoke it spilled and sprayed everywhere. The only time she took her fingers out was when I made a mistake and then she'd slap my hands, leaving a long slippery streamer stretching from her mouth to her hands and then to me. In the next room, behind the sliding glass doors, sat her sick husband, Mr Coombes.

I hardly ever saw him close up. He was the fuzzy shape through the glass who made the house shake with his coughing. Mr Coombes was emphysemic. He'd cough so deep that I thought his lungs would be dragged up and pop out on to his lap, for sure. Then he'd wheeze and they'd be sucked in again, ready for next time. Sometimes he'd come to the door in his dressing gown and flannelette pyjamas to talk to Mrs Coombes. It was really sad and everything but I couldn't be too sympathetic. I was too busy rubbing the saliva from my hands and working on the fingering for 'Baa Baa Sheep' before she got back. I lasted two terms with the Coombes before I packed up my nursery rhymes and went back to pumping out medleys from *South Pacific* on the pianola. I thought that maybe ballet was the answer.

Judy Miller left school early two days a week to go into the city for ballet. Judy was tall and thin and walked differently from everyone else. She was like a puppet whose head string was a bit shorter than all the others. It was called 'good posture' and she got it from dancing. She had a little vanity case with ballerinas on the front and she wore her hair tied up in a bun. Judy was the new leader of the neat girls.

Mum said I could take lessons too but I wouldn't get a vanity case until I'd gone at least a year and I couldn't travel into town. I went to the library and found a notice for Saturday classes held in the Masonic Lodge at Hurstville.

MISS CORALIE COOMBES
TEACHER OF CLASSICAL
AND MODERN DANCE

It was probably a coincidence. I arrived at the hall with my new tutu and satin shoes tucked in Dad's old airline bag and searched for the teacher. She was obviously amongst all the mothers who were sitting and knitting along one wall, but they all looked alike. Bad sign. There wasn't a Margot Fonteyn amongst them. Worse, on close investigation, there *was* a Coombes. She was young and thin and her fingers were dry but there was a fat, damp lady seated at the piano on stage and rumbling coughs were coming from the store room in the back. Things looked bad from the beginning.

For a start, there were no beams or mirrors like a real dance school and I wasn't allowed to wear my tutu or pointe shoes. Miss Coombes said they were the things ballerinas had to earn. She said I wouldn't go on to my toes until I'd mastered all the basics in the beginner's course and it could take years.

That wasn't a problem for the other participants. They had plenty of time. The oldest was probably only six years old. They were all decked out in tiny leotards, black jiffies and coloured headbands. A couple even had pierced ears. I stood at the back in my shorts and socks and had a pretty clear view of both Coombes over the heads of the midgets. It was painful—the midgets were good. They could face the front and still have a toe pointed squarely at both side walls. It was a freak show of double-jointed midgets masquerading as children. I picked up my tutu and never went back. It was becoming very clear that neat girls got off to an early start.

It was the same with tennis. Mum said I could start so I found a court, booked my lesson and was aced by a five-year-old the first day I went. I was too old for the Brownies and too young for the Drum Majorettes. I tried gymnastics. The RSL ran it at the School of Arts but every night at nine you had to stop mid-way through a forward roll or reverse somersault to face the front and recite the pledge. The lights would go down and a fluorescent cross would come on over the stage. 'At the going down of the sun, and in the morning, we will remember them.' Then back to the mat to pick up where you left off.

By the end of fifth class I had tried every notice on the library board and the evidence of my failure was filling up the house. Rhonda's old glory box was packed with racquets and tutus and gym boots and yoga mats. The yoga was Mum's idea. She went on Wednesday afternoons with the ladies from the golf club. Everyone was old like Mum and they weren't serious about the exercises at all. They'd roll their bottoms over their heads for the reverse high lotus and little farts would pop out. It was contagious, like a yawn. One would come and then there'd be pops and giggles everywhere. And no one was embarrassed except me.

I probably would have given up if it wasn't for Mr Henley, next door. He was the only person who had any faith in me. He was always encouraging. 'Stand up straight, Moya. Round shoulders do not a Miss Australia make.' Mr Henley knew about things like that. He listened to music that didn't have any words, was a member of the Rockdale Historical Society and his niece Deirdre taught physical culture.

Physical culture or 'physie' was a cross between dancing and gymnastics. It was the poor girl's ballet and I took to it like a duck to water. Basically, it was marching and exercises. The marching was most important and you could tell a good physie team by its corner-turning. It was a high spin pivoting movement and the best corner-turner generally got to be captain. In my first year it was Jenny Sealey. She'd dropped ballet and picked up physie after the ant episode and now that she was captain she thought she was really crash hot again.

She led the team as it marched around the hall. We had to keep in time and do everything that the captain did. This was pretty boring with Jenny because she was really uninspired and only did what the teacher told her to. I knew I would be much better if only I had the chance. I just had to wait for the right moment.

I was put in the front line for the exercises because Deirdre, our teacher, said I was very well balanced. This was the best position and there was a lot of fighting about it. Especially amongst the mothers. They sat up the back and argued all the time. About what colour leotards we should wear and if Deirdre was as good as the teacher from Hurstville Branch and whether the front line would crack under pressure in the state competitions. They were particularly worried about me because my lateral bends were still a bit shaky and I was an unknown quantity. Deirdre was sticking her neck out by giving me a chance.

I practised secretly every day. Partly for Deirdre but mainly to become the first girl ever to develop an alternative to the pivot. By the time the comps came around I was ready.

It was risky. The team was dressed to kill, with lipstick and eyeshadow and special fake tan smeared on our legs. A couple of the girls were wearing little foam rubber bras to give them shape and all the mothers sat in the audience desperate for us to win. The team before us had done really well. The judging panel were impressed. The music started and we were on.

Jenny led the pack. She was four girls ahead of me and was approaching her second turn when my first corner came up. This was it. I dropped to the floor, swivelled on my knees, did a forward roll and cartwheeled back into line. It was a spectacular turn. I caught sight of Deirdre on the sidelines and she was amazed. I was spurred on. At the next corner I sprung a reverse lotus into a backward somersault and would probably have finished with a back flip if two of the mothers hadn't dragged me off the floor with their bare hands. They were screaming and shouting, and Mrs Sealey was the worst. She kept going on and on about the old Topsy Amanda episode and me being a nigger lover. Deirdre was crying and I didn't get to be captain after all. I was exhausted. I had come to the end of the line.

My last months at Bexley Primary were spent quietly. I made the odd visit to recorder lessons and old-time dance but my heart wasn't in it. It was just as well I had the exams to think about.

Everyone in sixth class had to do a special test to determine which high school you went to. The top of the tree was St George Girls High which was selective and took the brightest girls from the whole district. If you didn't get in, you had to go to one of the co-ed schools like Kogarah or Kingsgrove which were rough and full of molls. The girls there wore their uniforms hitched up around their bottoms and the boys wore brightly-coloured socks. The idea of going co-ed was really frightening and we knew only a few of us would escape. I hadn't spoken to a boy since I left Glebe and that was nearly four years before. Luckily, the memory was still strong enough to make me try really hard in the test.

The teachers made a ceremony out of the results. We assembled in the hall, sang the national anthem and waited. The names were read out in alphabetical order. By the time Miss Cornish got to S I could barely hear my school for all the crying going on. Little groups of girls were sobbing and screaming and hanging on to the legs of their class teachers. It was incredible. 'Moya Sayer. St George.'

I was so happy I didn't even care about the next result. 'Jenny Sealey. St George.' I had been saved once more and this time Dad had nothing to do with it. My friend Rosalie was going too and virtually all the neat girls. It was a triumphant new beginning.

The Tadpole

With my enrolment just weeks away, I spent the Christmas holidays planning my entry into the new world. The way I saw it, you had to trust your instincts and my instincts told me to trust the neat girls. They wanted to do well and they knew the best ways to go about it. Like the new uniform. I definitely wanted chisel-toe school shoes and store-bought tunics for a start. I knew you could tell a home-made job a mile off, mainly by the unevenness of the reinforced stitching. Mum's instincts were different. She still had a lot of Glebe in her and this led to fights.

She'd always copied the tunics in the shop. We'd go up to Hurstville and try them on as if we were going to buy. Then Mum would whip out her tape measure in the dressing room, measure the width of the skirt and the length of the bodice and run one up on the Singer. They always looked different because she'd buy better-quality material or not be neat enough with the stitching. I told her I wouldn't be caught dead with one of hers this time and she said, 'Blind Freddy'd be glad to see it.' So then I said they just weren't good enough which really got Dad's back up.

'Keep going with these bloody airs and graces and you won't start St George at all, no bloody risk about that.'

He said I was turning into a snob. In our family there was only one thing worse than being unmarried and pregnant and that was being stuck up. Dad's business was doing pretty well by then, but you'd never know it. He still drove the old ute and Mum wore her new diamond ring turned into the palm of her hand. They were petrified of putting on the dog.

Anyway, Dad said he'd write to the government and get my school changed, so I decided it wasn't worth the risk. Mum took extra care with the stitching and I stood firm about the chisel-toe Ponytails, just managing to avoid the round-toe models with the bear tracks in the heel. And I demanded a leather briefcase instead of a cardboard Globite. I got regulation Cottontail panties, a panama hat, gloves, a tie and a blazer. Everything was navy except for red and white trims on the hat and tie. It was pretty old-fashioned compared to the co-ed schools but it made you look neat and very intelligent, that's for sure. I felt like a completely new person.

I tried on the uniform every morning in the holidays just for practice and packed and repacked the briefcase. My biros were new, my homework book was covered in brown paper and heavy, expensive plastic, and the zipper on my new pencil case worked perfectly. I was all set.

I'd practised with the uniform so often that on the big day I was dressed in four and a quarter minutes. I had to wait on the verandah for hours. I sat with my briefcase by my feet and my panama on my lap and, as soon as the sun came up, Mum brought me out a special breakfast on a tray. Dad washed the Morris while she got ready. We had a fight about what she should wear. She wanted her flatties and I had my heart set on the high-heel patents. She'd had her hair done the day before and in her good dress and stilettos she looked perfect.

And then we got lost. Not on the way to St George because we'd marked the route in the Gregory's. But inside. It was so big. Somehow we found our way to the front foyer. It was beautiful there. The floor was patterned in lino and the walls were covered with polished wood lists of distinction and boards of merit. The names were written in gold. Mum was just telling me how I would be up there one day when a voice came bellowing from behind us.

'Madam, madam, please remove yourself. Your stilettos are damaging my dragon.'

The voice was low and well-rounded and sounded just like someone on the ABC. It came out of a small, grey-haired woman with bowed legs, bent body and flashing eyes. She had a gold pen handing from a chain around her neck, a notebook in her hand and sensible shoes on her feet. The shoes looked sus-piciously like the ones I had rejected, the ones with bear tracks in the heel. It was the headmistress, Miss Pickwright.

'You are standing on our history.'

Mum was. The brightly-coloured lino formed a picture of St George slaying the dragon. It was the school crest and my mother was standing right in the middle of it. Miss Pickwright held out her hands to confiscate the high heels and recited the rules. We had broken about half a dozen before I'd even enrolled. No student is allowed in the foyer without a note, no person is to walk over or near the crest, no person is to wear metal-tipped stilettos on school ground.

'And, our girls never, ever, wear chisel-toe shoes.'

We were obviously failing Miss Pickwright's strict guidelines and she hadn't even got past our feet. I stuck out my chest so she could at least take note of the neatness of Mum's stitching, but it wasn't any good. She wrote my name in her little pad and took another good look at Mum. It was pathetic. Squeezed up against the wall on the edge of the famous crest, Mum looked ridiculous in her stocking-toe feet. From that moment I realised our family was going to be out of its depth.

I was put into 1D. That wasn't because of Mum and the stilettos, though, it was alphabetical. I was incredibly disappointed. Not only was I saddled with Jenny Sealey again but also being in D made you feel inferior. The girls in 1A did better from the word go. They got the best teachers and they seemed to be a lot smarter than everyone else. They had names like Adams and Beasley and they were the girls Miss Pickwright praised in her morning messages over the public address system. She'd sit in her office and croon to her girls (pronounced 'gels') from a microphone on her desk.

'My beautiful, wonderful gels. You will not sort files, you will not pound typewriters. You will have brass plates on your doors. You are the *creme de la creme* and I love you.'

She would interrupt lessons whenever she had some good news.

'My wonderful, intelligent gels. I cannot wait to tell you. Two little tadpoles from Class 1A will debate in the district competitions. I am so very, very proud.'

All the 'gels' in first year were tadpoles. If you worked hard enough you eventually got to be a frog or even a Black Cat. The Black Cats were a special club Miss Pickwright formed to encourage ingenuity. If you came up with a new idea then you got a special cat brooch for your blazer. The better you did at St George the more brooches you had on your lapel. You could even get one years after you left if you joined a profession and had your name on a door. This was the Brass Plate Club. There were prefects and class captains, and the cream of the crop from all forms was called the Sixty. By second term Sarah Adams was one of the Sixty and I was still badgeless. I knew I had it in me to be a Black Cat, though, if only I could come up with one good idea. I just had to wait for my moment.

'You dirty, dirty gels.'

Miss Pickwright came in whenever she had bad news, too.

'You dirty, filthy gels. Two old Paddle Pop

wrappers are flying around the playground. *Two!* The tennis courts will be closed for a week, the trampoline is now out of bounds and Paddle Pops have been banned from the canteen for the rest of term.'

Miss Pickwright knew how to hit where it hurt the most. And she did. She was particularly ruthless when her joints were playing up. She was tormented by an arthritic condition that was gradually twisting her body into swollen knots. The arthritis slowed her down but it never stopped her altogether.

'You depraved, unintelligent whores. You don't deserve a place in this school. Assembly Hall. Immediately.'

Someone had been caught at something and she was going to tell us, in a spotlight from the centre stage.

A Black Assembly.

The curtains were drawn. The hall was dark. The teachers sat in a semicircle behind the microphone and looked as frightened as us. It could easily be one of them.

Margaret Denton and Sharon Wilson had been found by the stationmaster at Kogarah, smoking cigarettes and talking with boys. It was rumoured that they were not wearing either their hats or their gloves at the time. As soon as the names were called out, the 632 girls who weren't caught breathed out, sucked in their cheeks and promptly decided that Margaret and Sharon were rough and probably molls. The two girls were dragged sobbing on to the stage where they were divested of every skerrick of red and white from their uniforms. Their faces were slapped and they weren't allowed to wear their hats for a fortnight.

None of this was new to me because Miss Pickright and I had obviously read the same books. It had happened at Miss Princey's in Durham when Sheila Withington stole pocket-money from blazers in the cloak room and at Sussex School for Girls after a particularly noisy midnight feast. Miss Pickwright worked really hard to make our public school seem more private every day.

Like uniform inspection. Miss Shark, the deputy, would see to that. She wore a little pair of scissors around her neck and tore down any hemline that was found to be more than three inches from the ground when kneeling. She'd flick up our skirts with her fountain pen to examine our bottoms for regulation Cottontails. She was obsessed with us and would hide crouched behind a big poinsettia tree to watch for hatless girls on the walk from the station. Miss Shark had obviously read the same books as Miss Pickwright. A lot of the teachers had. The staffrooms were filled with ancient women sprouting hair on their chins, handkerchiefs from their cardigans and soft, white English flesh from stockings that stopped at the knees.

Standards were high, but the rot set in with 'equal opportunity' when the staff was sprinkled with a few token males. These 'gentlemen' were carefully screened by Miss Pickwright beforehand and were so straight they made Mr Chipps look like a child molester. But still, straight or not, they had 'flies' and 'male swells' and the sight of a urinal being installed was pretty exciting. We talked about scrotums and penises and whether his wife liked 'it' until Parka Joe took all the mystery away.

Parka Joe gave me my first look at a male thing. Well, not just me. All the girls on the 3:30 from Kogarah to Rockdale got to see Parka Joe's penis at some time or another. As soon as the train passed the Bentley Street signal box he'd slip his parka off his lap and stare straight ahead. It hung out of his overalls like a flabby pink nose, fat and soft-looking. For a long time I thought it was bandaged, but Pam Henderson said they were all like that. And she was in a position to know.

She'd sit opposite Joe deliberately and laugh out loud as soon as he moved his jacket. Pam was my new friend. She wasn't that smart but her sister had been. That's how Pam got into St George in the first place. There was a special ruling that allowed the family of 'old girls' to enrol even if they didn't pass all the tests. It made Pam feel inferior. She was a trouble-maker in class from the start. She had long, brown legs, a beautiful body and looked at least fifteen. She was what Mum called an 'early developer'.

Not like me. The other girls were popping breasts while I couldn't even manage a pimple on my chin. They got to use the only toilet in the block with a floor-to-ceiling door. It was the one with the incinerator and a little sink in the corner. They'd disappear carrying a little oblong plastic bag with pink flowers on it and stay in there for ages performing their secret ritual with solemnity. If your hormones weren't on the move you'd be out of the toilets in ten seconds flat. It was humiliating because everyone knew.

I'd go into the cubicle to check my white Cotton-tails. Sometimes, two or three times a day. Nothing. I'd pound my stomach. Nothing. The incinerator itself was a constant reminder because the smell of burning sanitary pads reached into every crevice of the school. I wanted to be a part of it and for a while I'd slide tissues into the tray just to get the practice. I wasn't fooling anyone, though, because my skin was perfect.

The breast-poppers had acne and got to use Clearasil. As soon as their faces were covered in pimples boys started ringing them up. And then of course it was time to visit David Jones corsetry department.

The old pigeon-chested brassiere advisors would take them into brocade cubicles with gold carpet and dainty, velvet stools with wrought-iron legs. Mother would sit on the stool while the pigeon performed the fitting. Bending from the waist she'd give a demon-stration of how to wear the garment properly. She'd shove a knarled hand deep into her C-cup, pull up a big flabby breast and then push it in again. The breast-poppers were really impressed by the whole procedure and from then on, after PE, I'd have to stand in my singlet and watch them. They'd reach into their bras, find their mounds, pull them up and then push them down. The breast-poppers invariably came from blond-brick homes.

Rich girls had faster-acting hormones. 'Rich' was any girl whose house had venetian blinds, a double garage and blond bricks. In the 1960s 'blond' meant new and 'new' meant rich. They lived down the line at Blakehurst or Sylvania Waters and their fathers were usually assistant managers at some branch of the Commonwealth Bank. When long blond hair came in the rich girls were ready for it. Girls like me, from dark-brick houses, had just got razor cuts. *They* wore dresses from Merivale to the school dances and ate yogurt for lunch. Dark-brick girls sewed Simplicity patterns and prayed for our hormones to start working so we could put on weight and then diet on yogurt. The rich girls never had anything to do with kids like me. It sounds incredible but they wouldn't even have anything to do with the neat girls.

I'd backed the wrong horse. The neat girls were just small time at St George. For a start, in high school, you did essays not projects so the Derwents were useless and the rich girls had moved way past pencils anyway. They had special Texta felt pens that didn't show through to the other side of the page. Girls who I'd thought knew everything, like Jenny Sealey and the Bexley ballerina, Judy Miller, were struggling just to keep their heads above water. And I was so low down on St George's evolutionary scale that I wasn't even a tadpole. I was an amoeba.

An amoeba with braces. Mr Stanley, the dentist, had tried everything, but my teeth were just too big. He started by extracting my six-year-old molars and would have got stuck into the wisdom teeth too if I hadn't stopped him. For a start, I knew that if I was going to do well at St George I'd need all the wisdom

I could get. And, secondly, I wasn't sure about his motives. He said my molars had the biggest root system he'd ever come across. He kept them in a bottle in his cabinet. It was possible he just wanted my other teeth to get his name in a journal.

Anyway, he sent me off to Mr Box, the orthodontist in Macquarie Street. Mr Box was the cleanest man I had ever met. He must have washed his hands in disinfectant ten or fifteen times a day and you could always smell him coming. He was really fat and so short that he had to stand on a platform just to see into your mouth. He had beautiful teeth though and all his own. Mum said they were a credit to him. On the other hand, all the nurses wore braces which she said were probably a perk of the job.

I started off with a night brace. It was a metal contraption that clicked into your back teeth and then ran outside your cheeks to a sponge tied at the back of your head. It made you look like a grid-iron player in America. I never wore it and Mr Box could tell. He'd stick his Pine-o-Cleen fingers into my mouth and go crook on me for being slack. The day he told me the night brace wasn't working and the real braces would have to go on, he was ecstatic. Maybe because he loved a challenge or maybe because he thought I deserved to suffer. They were installed top and bottom with tiny elastic bands joining both jaws.

Mum took me to see *The Sound of Music* the day I got them in. She thought Julie Andrews would be an inspiration because she had such good teeth herself. And then every two months after I'd been for a 'tightening' she'd take me to see another show. Mum knew how much the braces hurt. Mr Box would screw the wires so tight that I couldn't eat a finger-bun for days. And then, when I could eat, I was always finding soggy bits of devon sandwich stuck in the metal. I put cotton wool in my cheeks to stop the sharp edges gouging great holes in the flesh and the devon stuck to that too. It was pretty disgusting and made me very self-conscious at the school dances. Pam and I went together.

As an early developer Pam's hormones had been jumping for years and all the boys could tell. She was very popular and always deserted me to pash with her partner during the last set. I danced in a circle with the other nice, neat girls. My mother still made all my clothes. She'd send me off in pintucks and velvet bows and wonder why I cried all the way home in the Holden.

But I knew the Sydney Tech boys could tell a nice girl a mile off and that's where they stayed. For a while I put it down to my braces, but at one dance I kept my mouth tightly shut for three hours and by the time I decided to try smiling instead, my mother was outside in the Holden and Pam had a love bite.

It wasn't her first, either. Her boyfriend met her after the swimming carnival and gave her one behind the kiosk. She told her mother it was a water burn because she'd swum the 200 metres so fast. Her mother was so proud she took a Polaroid straight away. Her father tore up the Polaroid and grounded Pam for a month. But then Mr Henderson was pretty worldly for Bexley. He wore Italian shoes without any laces, owned a baby-bootee factory and wouldn't read the afternoon papers. They lived in a dark-brick house, but it had one of those Cape Cod conversions to put his old mother in. This made Pam 'nouveau Cod', just one step behind blond brick. And I was one step behind that again.

I was still looking for a good idea to get me into the Black Cats. The Americans landed a man on the moon and I was inspired. We watched the first moon walk on television sets in the assembly hall. It was so exciting that a lot of the girls cried. Miss Pickwright said it was the beginning of the Age of Discovery and her 'gels' would take an essential part. That afternoon I walked into her office and shared my good idea.

It was a mouse launch and Miss Pickwright was right behind me. Miss Condies, the science mistress, gave me her favourite mouse, Pablo. He'd been with St George for a long time and did quite a few tricks, including breeding.

It was a simple investigation involving the effect of G-forces on small rodents but it took a lot of preparation. I bought a distress signal rocket from a ships' supplier and made the capsule from an old pepper container. My plan was for Pablo to be attached to the rocket and after take-off a small firecracker would blow the capsule free, releasing a tiny parachute and floating Pablo back to earth.

I got police permission for the explosion and Miss Pickwright invited the local press to cover the event. She always liked her girls to get the publicity they deserved. I got the choir organised to sing the

71

school song and the drama club to practise special chants, like in America.

> 2...4...6...8...
> Aussie mouse goes into space
> Get...set...ready...go...
> We all love the brave Pablo.

It was incredibly exciting. But before I go on I must say this. The health and welfare of Pablo was uppermost in my mind the whole time. What happened was just one of those unavoidable tragedies.

It was a beautiful day, no wind, perfect conditions for a launch. The school assembled on the oval while we prepared Pablo for flight. Miss Condies administered the anaesthetic but I don't think it was enough because when I put him into the capsule he sneezed twice. I suppose there must have been a bit of pepper left at the bottom where his head went.

The cheer leaders were doing a good job at getting the crowd excited and Pam gave a special commentary over the loud speakers...

'It's a great day for Australia. I can see Moya Sayer consulting with scientist Miss Condies...all seems to be going well...the crowd...terrific response...a first for...overwhelming...'

Miss Pickwright gave a speech about initiative, the man from the newspaper took my photo and I lit the rocket. One second it was there, the next, ka... boom, it was like a gun going off. I thought it would start slowly like at Cape Canaveral but it shot off so fast that you couldn't follow it at all.

Then a sixth former spotted something smoulder·
ing on the far edge of the grounds. The rocket had
ploughed across six feet of ground and was just a mol-
ten lump by the time we got there. The parachute never
opened. Pablo didn't have a chance. It only took two
days for Sarah Adams to report me to the RSPCA.

I tried to make it better by erecting a little Paddle
Pop cross where the rocket landed, but the hockey
team ran it down on the first day. I had said a prayer
over it too, with Chris Shackleton, the leader of the
Inter School Christian Fellowship.

I refused to give up. I tried and failed and tried
again. Like with Charity Week. The girl who raised
the most money got to join the Sixty. The girl with
the most unusual idea got to be a Black Cat. I went
for the Cat and decided to be a shoe-shiner like I'd
seen on American movies. I got a kit together and
made up a special Negro mask from a pair of black
winter stockings. I cut holes for my eyes and nose
and weaved the other stocking into a long plait.
With a head scarf I looked suspiciously like Topsy
Amanda. I gave a free rendition on one knee of
'Swannee River' or 'Mammy' with every shine. I was
a big hit. Then Miss Pickwright walked past me in
the corridor and I said, 'Hey, bosslady, you wanna
shine from a poor nigger gal? Ten cents iz all.'

She pulled the stocking from my head, slapped me
over the ear and said I was racist. I had to give back
all the money I had earned. I was really upset mainly
because I had no idea what a racist was. I asked Miss
Pickwright and she slapped me over the other ear and
said I was insolent as well.

Miss Pickwright was very unpredictable like that. Chris Shackleton came undone when she tried a new way to encourage the students to go to the ISCF meetings. She got up in assembly and asked the school to repeat things that she said in Chinese. The girls laughed but they said them all the same. Then Chris told them that they'd all just promised to go to next Friday's meeting.

It was a great ruse and a triumph for Chris until Miss Pickwright hit her across the back of the head and took over the microphone. She said Chris had used mind control, just like the Nazis. She said we were all sheep to say things when we didn't know what they meant.

Apart from the badge failures, I wasn't doing too badly. In second year I was put into the A class for everything except art and music. I didn't have any illusions about those two subjects anyway. The art mistress had told me I couldn't draw the first day I went and Miss Bell, in music, wrote 'No ear for this subject' on my term report. I was sorry I wasn't any good at art because I really enjoyed it, but I didn't like music. The lessons were always the same. Miss Bell would put on a classical record and you were supposed to write what it was about. The other girls would say 'a walk through a German forest at dawn' or 'a leaf travelling down a babbling brook' but it didn't mean anything to me. It was impossible to be sure when the composer hadn't bothered to write words to it and I'd never been into a German forest, anyway. Neither had anybody else, including Miss Bell. And I got very low marks for writing that

Beethoven's Fifth reminded me of Hurstville bowling alley on a Saturday night. It did, too.

Mum and Dad played there in a team competition. They were the All Stars and Mum really enjoyed it because it was good exercise for the fat on the top of her legs. The fat had started to build up when we moved away from the two-storey house at Glebe. Mum said all that running up and down the stairs had kept her in shape. She'd lost it again during Rhonda's tragedy but not for long. She tried a lot of things to get the weight down, like Ford Pills and 5BX exercises. She'd walk up and down the verandah on her bottom and slap her legs together while she watched the telly, which really annoyed Sue. She even tried Silhouette which was a gym at Hurstville. She was up there slapping her thighs on the floor one Saturday morning, while I sat very still at home.

My hormones were on the move at last. It was a hot summer day and I was getting ready for the beach. Dad was the only person at home and I couldn't tell him. When Mum finally came home she checked my panties and gave me an oblong plastic bag with pink flowers on it, a little elastic belt and a book called *So Now You're a Woman*.

The book stressed feminine hygiene and sexual caution. I wasn't allowed to have a bath or lift anything heavy and I couldn't go swimming because I was 'unwell'. I raced to the chemists for a tube of Clearasil and sat by the phone. I waited two and a half years.

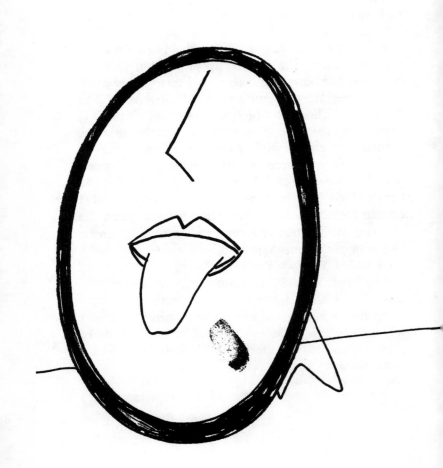

5

The Tongue Kiss

Those two and a half years were filled with some pretty memorable pimples and a stream of Tween-Age training brassieres. I never managed to get past the trainers. For years my breasts were more like two small fried eggs than anything else. By the time they finally exploded to 32A, the women's movement was in full swing and the only good bra was a burnt one.

Meanwhile, the suburbs were changing fast and things I'd only dreamt of through *Father Knows Best* and *Donna Reid* were bursting into dark-brick homes from one end of Sydney to the other. Our place too. Suddenly 'Mom' had a station wagon, instant coffee and thick paper bags full of gallon containers of icecream balanced on both hips. I thought the plastic icecream containers were the ultimate in American sophistication, but their chocolate chip chic didn't last long. Within weeks Mum was sticking psychedelic Contact all over them and selling them as cottonwool ball holders at the golf club fete. The great Contact cover of the suburbs had begun.

She bought it at Roselands. You could get everything there and park your station wagon under concrete cover while you did it. Roselands threw us into a frenzy. It was a wonderland, a shopper's Disneyland. Every Saturday morning I'd go with Pam and Chris Shackleton to hang around the Raindrop Fountain and eat lunch at the Four Seasons Self-Service. It was incredible; you could get sweet and sour pork, coleslaw and pavlova, all on the one tray.

Peter Stuyvesants came in tens. We'd smoke them on Roseland's Japanese bridge sometimes. It was beautiful there. They'd even built a special pond underneath to make it more authentic. It was a little bit of Japan between the car parks. A girl from school said her father designed it. He was a draughtsman, so maybe he did. Anyway, it was nice to suck on the Stuyvos, stand on the bridge and think about that. Or about other things, like the school special.

Chris and I caught the special 472 every afternoon. It didn't travel anywhere near where we lived but it did pick up the boys from Marist Brothers. We had to run the last block along Harrow Road so we'd have time to spray on some Avon Rapture and decide what we were going to say before it arrived. The boys got on two stops later, swaggered down the aisle, threw their Globites at our feet and opened the windows to get rid of the Rapture smell. They always ignored us but they knew we were there all right. They'd talk in loud voices about the football results and the brown-eye that got Johnson six of the best. (The best?) We'd say 'Bye' when we got out and as the bus was pulling away, their heads would stick out of the windows and we'd hear... 'Hey, are youse comin' to tha?' Tha what? Tha what?

It was frustrating, but the long walk back gave us plenty of time to think about it. And we'd talk every night on the phone as well. I had a pretty strict routine. I'd get home, talk to the dog, look in the fridge, get changed into my pyjamas, look in the fridge, write in my diary, look in the fridge, talk to Mum, check the fridge again, and then get on the phone to Chris before tea. Dad could never understand how much we had to discuss and so there were always fights. There were fights with my sister Sue, too, usually about her Rapture. It was pretty strong and took so long to wear off that she generally knew I'd pinched it. I took a lot of her stuff, I just couldn't keep my hands off it. Or my feet.

'Mum, Mum...Moya's worn my sling-backs.'

'I did not.'

For once, Mum was on my side. 'How would she fit her big clodhoppers into them? She couldn't.'

I could...*and* I had the blisters to prove it.

I took her clothes as well. Sue bought her own so she didn't have to put up with Mum's sloppy stitching. It wasn't easy, though. I had to sneak the gear out of the house and get changed in the shed at the bottom of the driveway. I kept a mirror there, and a little sewing kit to take the hems up. Sue might have had small feet, but she was a lot taller than me. She knew something was going on but she couldn't work out what. She had less trouble with the big Easter Rabbit that her boyfriend John had given her.

She kept it beside her bed to remind her of him. It had enormous ears and a big pink nose and was covered in beautiful coloured foil. It sat there for months and the temptation was just too great. I started eating little bits of chocolate from the base, and then off his paws and bottom, and I'd rearrange the foil so Sue didn't notice a thing. I should have left the ears. One day, she picked him up and the foil just crumpled in her fingers. She locked everything in Rhonda's old glory box after that, including the Rapture.

This was a real blow as I only had Pretty Peach which was a special scent for adolescents and not sexy at all. On the other hand, adult Avon was fantastic and it made really good Christmas presents. You didn't even have to go to the shops to get it. I always gave Dad Avon aftershave. He had a whole drawer full of bottles shaped like vintage cars and horses' heads and ocean liners. He said he liked it even though he never used any. It was like Sue's rabbit. He said the bottles were just too nice to open. I wouldn't have minded, I mean you could always fill them with coloured water when they were finished. I bought Dad the aftershave because I wanted him to be more sophisticated and genteel. I wanted him to be just like Stuart Wagstaff.

I was in love. Pam and I went to the Theatre Royal Saturday matinees six weeks in a row to see Mr Wagstaff in *There's a Girl in My Soup*. He played Robert Danvers, a fortyish connoisseur, wine-taster and girl-chaser, and he was fabulous. He was the most sophisticated man I had ever seen, a real Australian Cary Grant. Actually, he was a lot like Pam's father now that I think about it—no shoe-laces and mild manners. We waited at the stage door after every show and in the end I had twelve copies of his autograph (Pam didn't want hers).

He was a hard act to beat and the boys on the bus seemed pretty immature and coarse in comparison. But you had to settle for what you could get. We had lists of preference and you tried hardest for the boys at the top. I had six on mine, including Kevin, a butcher's apprentice; Barry, Sue's boyfriend's best friend; a Marist Brothers boy called Mark and a really cute guy who sold dress materials in David Jones. I never knew his name but his staff number was 88 and he had dark hair and was about nineteen. I also had Mr Wagstaff and Pam's father whom I secretly dubbed Mr X. But I wasn't really confident about getting either of them.

I had long- and short-term plans and I wrote them all in my diary. The long-term ones were the most challenging.

PLAN FOR ACTION:
ASSIGNMENT UGLY DUCKLING

	NOW	*AIM* (1970)
AGE:	15 YEARS 2 MONTHS	17 ONWARDS
HEIGHT:	5′ 4″	5′ 8″
WEIGHT:	8 ST 10 LBS	8 STONE ONLY
HAIR:	SHORT, WAVY	LONG, STRAIGHT
NAILS:	BITTEN	LONG
SKIN:	PIMPLY	EXCELLENT
TEETH:	COULD IMPROVE	WHITE, BRIGHT, FRESH

In the short term, I concentrated on Kevin, the butcher boy, and Sue's boyfriend's best friend,

Barry. Pam was going after Dave McCarthy. We used old Sally, the dog, as a decoy by taking her for long walks to the shops. With 2SM blaring from the trannies in our baskets, we'd walk five blocks out of the way, via the oval, Dave McCarthy's house and Barry's place, just in case they were hanging about the fence. They never were but Sally got lots of exercise which must have done her good. She turned to fat when I gave up on Barry and Pam decided Dave McCarthy was a deadhead anyway. Sally had already proven to be useless in my efforts to chat up Kevin, the butcher boy. My dog had this problem with butchers.

It was always the same. As soon as we were right outside Smith's Fine Meats, Sally would squat and do a big pooh on the footpath. There was no moving her once she'd started, so I'd just stand there feeling pretty helpless while Sally strained and Mr Smith screamed and threw his meat axe around on the other side of the window. Kevin moved away in 1968 when Mr Smith had a heart attack and the shop turned into a Lebanese take-away.

I turned my attentions to Mark, the boy on the bus. He was a cadet and every Friday he'd wear the uniform and carry a rifle. He never spoke, but you could tell he was intelligent and very sensitive. As soon as he got on I'd try to make eye contact with him, smiling the whole time. I got the idea from Mum. 'No one likes an unhappy girl, Moya.' She must have been right. One day Mark finally looked at me. His eyes stayed on mine for about ten seconds and then he got off the bus. It was the first encouragement I'd ever had and after that I liked Mark like nothing. I didn't have much time, though, because he was in sixth form and by the time he finally noticed me I only had thirty-seven bus trips left to win him. The problem was I wanted him so much that I got too choked up to speak. I wrote a special poem about it. I wrote a lot of poetry then, a verse for every boy on the list.

> Sunburnt and handsome the boy on the bus
> Enters my life each day
> But all I can do is giggle
> And think of things to say
> And although I never say them
> In my heart he answers back
> The sunburnt handsome boy on the bus
> In the tilted army hat.

It was hard. For a start, Pam reckoned that Tommy Hachett said that Mark said that he really liked Beverly Trudeau. Beverly was a rich girl at school who had long blond hair that was naturally straight. I had to iron mine with the Sunbeam Steam and Dry. Also she had sex appeal, just like Pam. I would have done anything to have it but I didn't know where to start.

We were doing mammals in science and Miss Condies said that in the animal world it all boiled down to how you smelt. Apparently animals find their partners by sniffing them out. I gave up the Avon straight away and as soon as my natural smells got a chance to work, Mark spoke. On the nineteenth trip, he said 'Hi'. On the twentieth he said, 'Hi' and

'Bye', and on the twenty-first he said he didn't really like Beverly at all and was sorry that he'd asked her to the cadet passing-out parade dance. *He* was sorry! Anyway, then he asked me to go with him 'and-Tommy-Hachett-and-Tommy-Hatchett's-girlfriend-and-her-cousin-from-Cobar-to-see-a-movie-and-have-some-tea-after'. That night Mum got out all the Simplicity patterns to find a style for my first date dress.

The movie was a rerun of *Summer Place* and we held hands from the middle of the short, *Our Boys in Vietnam*, right up to the bit in the film where Troy Donohue gets the girl in trouble. We had sweet and sour pork and Mateus rosé at the Green Jade. Mark paid and on the verandah he kissed me four times and asked me 'down the National Park next Sunday'.

I spent the week imagining how it would be. Mark was a Heathcliff and I was a Cathy. There were brooding eyes, white cotton shirts and soft winds blowing across the moors. But on the big day, Mark took off his ACI Glass T-shirt and had shocking acne all over his back. I nestled my head in his armpit and the BO was unbelievable. If this was animal scent I was going back to Avon! Things got worse when he told me how much he liked me. I went off him straight away. I mean, what's the point? After that I started catching the train again.

The train had its drawbacks because I never got to meet any boys. Not counting Parka Joe. I had to spend Friday nights at home again watching the movie with my mother and eating Rocky Road to the hum of Mum's steel-wool pads as she polished her golf clubs ready for ladies' day. Mum would sit on the Jason recliner and I would take the pouf. Dad would listen to the trots in the kitchen and every time a race came on he'd turn it up so loud that you couldn't hear anything. Dad owned trotters himself then and raced them in country meetings or at Harold Park if they were good enough. The most promising one was a little mare called Lady Nelson. She won all her races in Bathurst and Wollongong and was considered to be a certainty for her first run in the city. She was a tiny horse with a lot of courage. But not enough. On the home turn at Harold Park she was penned in by a particularly large and aggressive stallion. No matter how hard Lady tried she couldn't get out, and the stallion edged her further and further against the rails. She lost the race and never had the will to win again. Mum and Dad said the experience had broken her heart. She was like all the other trotters my father ever had. They looked good but when it came to the crunch, they were just too sensitive.

So, all in all, the nights at home were pretty depressing. Rhonda and Bob had moved into their semi at Gladesville by then and Sue was always out with her new boyfriend, John, who was at the university. I was left by myself and either watched telly or wandered around the house trying to think of a way to get out. Dad said I was just like a colt straining at the reins. And he knew.

When John and Sue came home from a date they'd stand on the verandah and pash for ages. I could hear them in my bedroom because John was such a loud kisser. I used to lie in bed praying for them to stop so Sue wouldn't have an accident like Rhonda's. Mum was worried about it too and found excuses to check up on them. She started painting things like the letterbox to keep her eye on them. She liked painting. She said it gave life a lift.

'Excuse me, loves, this won't take a minute.'

Sue and John were pashing on the lounge when Mum burst in with a little pot of gold paint in her hand. She checked them out while she slapped a fresh coat of gold on the brown gas heater. Then she was gone again with, 'That looks better, doesn't it?'

Sue said she nearly died of embarrassment and if that wasn't bad enough, John got gold all over his new suede jacket when she pashed him against the letterbox on his way out. He'd got Mystery Magenta on his jeans when she pashed him against the dog kennel the week before. Sue said it was just too much. She reckoned Mum didn't have to worry about John anyway because he respected her. He was a nice bloke. She met him at the Fellowship the second time she went.

I started doing the rounds of the local churches too. I was Church of England but the boys who went there were real mangles. The Baptists were okay but a bit strict so I went Presbyterian for a while.

It was unbelievable. About thirty kids met every Sunday before the service and the next Friday night we'd meet at Rockdale station in front of the milk bar and go off to Luna Park or Hurstville Bowls or Geraldine Richards' place for a barbecue. I wasn't too keen on the church part, but it was a good way to meet people. The head of the Fellowship was really cute. He was the guy everyone wanted because he was older and had a car. I was stoked. He was a really spiritual person.

He was also the first guy to stick his tongue in my mouth. It was at a church house-party in the mountains. I knew he was keen on me because I sat right next to him on the drive up and every time he changed gears he stuck his elbow into my ribs and kept it there. That night, as the mist was curling in on the huts, he asked me if I'd like to see his engine. He had an HQ Holden and put a rug over the motor when it got too cold. Anyway, we got to the car and he held me hard against the fender and stuck his tongue down my throat. Of course I went off him right away, partly because I got scared, but mostly because I knew he thought I was easy.

My mother called it 'wet mouth' or 'French kissing' and said it led to trouble. Bexley was suspicious of all things French then. I didn't taste quiche for years and Mum never gave way on pâté. Actually, it was a bit of a surprise that smorgasbords took off the way they did. Smorgasbords were Swedish and Sweden was even more frightening than France.

But, in subtle ways, our family was definitely freeing up. Mum wore beads and psychedelic kaftans and started painting flowers on the letterbox. Flower power was big news. Bob ripped the old tiger tail off his petrol cap and stuck Contact daisies on the rear windows instead. It was love and peace and revolution. Sue and John went to university parties on the North Shore where girls said 'Fuck', didn't wear bras and smoked marijuana. Mum took to using polyunsaturated margarine and cooking everything in the vertical grill. It was all incredible and pretty scary. The papers were full of three new killers all starting with a 'C': cholesterol, coronaries and cancer. People had always known about cancer but had never actually said the word out loud.

Dad didn't know 'what the bloody country was coming to'. He banned John and 'all the other bloody long-haired university louts' from the house. It was suddenly very quiet. Dad reckoned it was bad form to talk about sex, politics or bodily functions, and that meant you couldn't talk about anything. We started to eat dinner in front of the TV and watch other people discuss the things we weren't allowed to. Like that other big 'C' killer, conscription.

It mainly affected boys from poor suburbs who weren't extra smart, like Johnnie Herrington. If you were rich or very bright then you got to go to uni and the government let you off. Sydney was full of American soldiers on rest and recreation leave, called R&R. Some of them were black. And then, out of the blue, one of Sue's friends married a corporal (a white one) and moved to a mobile home in South Dakota. She wrote for a while, but no one's heard from her in years.

Anyway, in her very last letter she sent us a big packet of love beads from Haight-Ashbury in San Francisco. Mum wore them with a yellow poncho when we saw *Hair* at the Kings Cross Metro. We got front row seats and she nearly died when they took all their clothes off. She'd never had anyone but my father. I was even more surprised because I'd never had anyone at all. But it was hard to see very much. In the end the cast came down from the stage and got us up to dance to 'Let the Sun Shine'. They gave Mum a flower, she talked to a nearly-nude Negro and in the end she said they all seemed like very nice people.

Mum was pretty groovy really and liked to keep up with the times. She started using teabags, wearing slacksuits and had a radical hysterectomy. A lot of ladies got hysterectomies and breast removals so they could beat cancer to the punch. If you disappeared just a little, you could sometimes prevent disappearing altogether. That's what I found out from the ladies at Tony of Rome Hairdressing Salon. And they knew.

They'd had the lot. I worked at Tony's on Saturday mornings and the regular clients were always disappearing to hospital for a few weeks and then coming back with a little bit less of themselves than they had before. They wore tiny bags of millet in their bras where their breasts used to be and exchanged details of their ops under the dryers. It was pretty noisy with all the machines going at once and stories of tumours flying from one end of the salon to the other.

'So he said it should come out.'

'What?'

'Malignant. Riddled with it.'

'You're dry, Mrs Harris. You can come out now.'

'What? Right through her?'

'What?'

'Cheryl's ready for you now, Mrs Harris.'

'Ovaries, womb, the lot.'

'Poor little bugger.'

All in all, Tony's made me sick. Apart from all the tumour talk there were the shampoos themselves with dandruff and scalp eczema and chronic split ends. And some ladies had strange enormous head bumps that rolled under your fingers when you worked up a lather. I knew they were the new cancers just trying to get out.

'Give us lots of lacquer, love. I want it for Thursday.'

If you last that long.

Still, Tony's was a lot better than the other jobs I'd tried, like at Shipley's Chemist and the Groovy Girl Boutique.

All the girls at school wanted to work in a chemist because it was glamorous. At Shipley's, I got a white uniform and the chance to use all the make-up testers when it wasn't too busy. Mr Shipley said it was important to use as many as possible so you could give good advice. I tried day creams and night oils and the complete range of waterproof mascaras. Sometimes three or four at once. Mr Shipley said I was so keen I could take more products home to experiment further. I was very diligent but it was all for nothing. No one cared what I thought of the different brands anyway. Most of the customers wanted other things.

'So what do you reckon I can put on this?'

'This' was a filthy foot with Grand Canyon cracks in the heel. Francine Peters, a girl from school, slipped her thong off and made me look at the foot up close. Her friend, Belinda, wanted some cream for a colony of cold sores that covered her mouth and were creeping up her nasal passages. There were stinking babies' bottoms, eyes exploding in pig styes, ingrown toe nails and slow-healing scabs. Men showed me their hernias and women asked for tampons in loud voices. It was a far cry from my dreams of Chanel No. 5 and Revlon lip gloss but Mr Shipley fired me before I could quit. He said he couldn't keep me on because I was the worst advertisement for beauty products he'd even seen. All those testers had brought me out in shocking pimples and the water-proof mascara had reduced my eyelashes to stubble. One by one. Mr Shipley was pretty good about it really. He took my uniform back and gave me two free tubes of Clearasil. The next week he hired Beverly Trudeau. She kept the job for ages. For some reason rich girls seem to have smaller pores.

As soon as my acne cleared I got a job at the Groovy Girl Boutique, but I only lasted one day. The manageress took exception to me telling the clients they were fat. They were. Groovy Girl sold jeans. The customers would lie in the changing rooms and expect me to pull up the zippers with a coathanger while they squashed in their bellies with their fists. Then they'd prance around in front of the mirror, get another style from the racks and we'd have to pummel their bellies all over again. They looked dis-gusting and someone had to tell them. But apparent-ly that someone shouldn't have been me.

My friend Chris was really huge. It ran in the

family. Chris was so fat that she'd never been able to cross her legs. She had this real thing about food. She took sandwiches to bed with her every night. She didn't always eat them, though, it was just having them with her that was important. Her mother put a padlock on the fridge but it didn't do any good.

Mrs Shackleton was enormous herself and fought a constant battle against the bulge. One year she became so desperate that she had her jaws wired together so she could only eat liquids. The doctor knocked out one of her teeth so the straw could go in. Anyway, in three months she actually gained twenty pounds. Apparently she was cooking gigantic roast dinners, then putting the lot (including dessert) into the blender and drinking it in secret. She was written up in a medical journal.

No one likes a fat girl and the girls at school were really paranoid about it. There was even a club called Friends Against Fat. It met every Friday at lunchtime and mainly consisted of not eating lunch while you listened to lectures on yogurt and the many uses of cottage cheese. Beverly Trudeau thought it up and she got to be a member of the Black Cats because Miss Pickwright thought it was such a good idea. But Beverly wouldn't accept Chris as a member. She said she'd give the club a bad name. I could have joined because I only had a small problem with my thighs, but on principle I decided to go with Chris to the Weight Off Centre for adult ladies instead. The only problem was you had to be overweight by a certain amount to be accepted. I hid some of Dad's lead fishing sinkers in my trouser cuffs and clocked in with an extra two stone.

The ladies at the Weight Off Club had a poem and a special pig pen for any members who gained weight between meetings. The leaders would discuss the diets and the ladies would give testimonials about how they'd been tempted and managed to resist. The piggies sat on the floor in a child's play-pen and wrote slogans like 'A morsel through the lips, a lifetime on the hips', a hundred times in exercise books.

I thought it was all pretty sick but it seemed to do the trick for Chris. By the end of the month she'd lost so much weight that she was able to cross her legs. She burst into tears. She couldn't believe it when she first felt her pelvic bones. She'd thought they were tumours, for sure. Anyway, she probably would have won the Best Weight Loss award if I hadn't forgotten my lead sinkers for the final weigh-in. On the records, I'd 'lost' an astonishing twenty-nine pounds and the ladies took my photo and entered me for Weight Off Queen of the Year.

The nominations for school prefects were just around the corner providing Chris with added incentive to keep reducing. No fat girl had ever got a badge and we knew it. Every morning I took her for long runs in her brother's wet suit and she went to bed each night with Glad Wrap swathed around her thighs. She was obsessed. She kept running and sweating and just when she looked terrific, she collapsed. The chronic dehydration kept her in hospital, exhausted, for weeks and when the teachers made their selection for prefect nomination, not one of them gave her a thought. Not one.

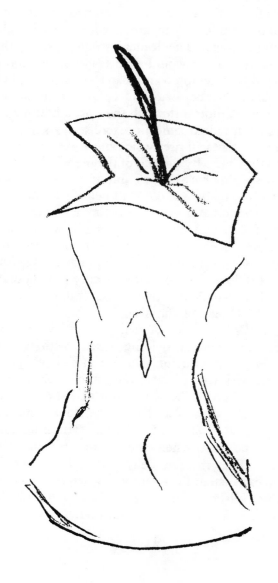

Sex
and a fruit compote

'My beautiful, wonderful gels. My *crème de la crème*, the staff has made its choice...'

At the end of fifth form Miss Pickwright announced the girls who had been selected to run for prefects and school captain. Chris was still in hospital and I was the only poor girl to make it. It looked like the last chance I'd have to get a badge for my empty lapel. There had been one other opportunity earlier in the year when I led the school debating team in the district competition but I blew it. The topic was 'Euthanasia is Evil' and I had no idea what it meant. (Euthanasia?...Youth in Asia??) We were speaking for the government and I led the team with an impassioned speech against adolescent prostitution in Bangkok. It was a really good speech but the opposition won and I never debated again. Or got a badge. I took up the campaign for prefect with a vengeance.

MOYA SAYER: THE BATTLERS' CHOICE

I wanted to appeal to the other poor girls and offer them some sort of representation. Everybody was sick of the rich girls anyway. They were chosen for everything because the teachers liked them best.

MOYA'S FOR YA: SAYER SAYS IT ALL

There was a great deal of discrimination in the nominations. Apart from everything else, only students attempting more than two first-level subjects in the Higher School Certificate were chosen to run. This disqualified a lot of girls from the start. First levels required discipline and fortitude and by the end of fifth form there were only a few students left in each subject. I nearly dropped out of modern history myself. The classes before school were really hard going. Half a dozen of us would cluster down the front around the heater. Mr Harrison would sit behind his desk and every so often he'd lift one side of his bottom to release a quiet burst of wind. The stench was incredible and with each lift from his chair we'd move further down the back of the room. Some days it was so bad we'd be right out in the corridor by the time the bell went. It was hard to hear but this wasn't too important because Mr Harrison always gave the same lesson. It was the one about Hitler hiding under his car in the Nazi riots against the Social Democrats. Mr Harrison loved this story and acted it out by jumping under the desk...'Nein, nein, ich bin nicht Adolf. Ich bin Franz.'

He taught ancient history too and then his favourite lesson was the battle techniques of the Spartans. He had tin soldiers that he'd set up in phalanx formation on the floor. Mr Harrison loved his soldiers; he'd been collecting them for thirty years. Apparently he was really disappointed when he was sent to an all-girl school. He thought we wouldn't appreciate the intricacies of the different uniforms and he was right. He tried hard, though, and often gave special after-school lessons to individual girls. If you joined him under the desk for the Hitler impersonation then you got very good marks. I'd showed enough interest in his phalanx to get his nomination for prefect.

There was no point even thinking about becoming captain. From our first day at school it was clear who would get that job. Sarah Adams. Her family was littered with old girls and her sister, mother and grandmother had all been school captains in the past. Even if Sarah had been a real dud she still would have got in. Miss Pickwright was really into tradition and in a public school you have to take whatever tradition you can get.

As it turned out, though, Sarah was no turkey. She was dux of the form every year and did so many first-level subjects that the teaching staff went on strike for overtime. Sarah was dark and pale like a Madonna. And very thin. She was queen of the rich girls without even trying because she had real class. She never spoke to me, except once in 1968 when I accidentally trod on her foot in assembly and she asked me to get off.

Sarah didn't put up any posters in the election campaign. Instead, she invited little groups of students to afternoon tea in Miss Pickwright's office and explained her policies personally. The ladies in the clerical department would serve tea and scones while Sarah and Beverly Trudeau, who was tipped for vice captain, shook hands at the door. I made my campaign speeches over a loud hailer in the playground and gave out little rubbers with my name written on them. And I organised an election disco at lunchtime with door prizes and free cordial and a special performance about what school would be like if I was prefect. It was a dance drama based on the French Revolution and set to John Lennon's 'Imagine'.

I explained my platform more fully at the pre-election assembly. I said I wanted to catapault St George into the twentieth century but basically it boiled down to hats. I'd done my research and I knew hats was a real vote-winner. I wanted them out and all the other girls did too. We were the only school left in the district to wear them and we felt like real dickheads in front of the boys. I gave a very funny speech which got lots of applause and some first form kids even started chanting my slogan, spontaneously. Just like that.

> At St George it's white and red,
> Vote for Moya, get bare heads.
> Yeah...Mo...ya.

It was incredible. Then the rich girls got up. They spoke quietly about what their school meant to them ...tradition, friendship, selectivity. They all wore their hats and when they'd finished they linked arms and sang the school song. Suddenly the whole school was on its feet, singing and crying and fishing out their beat-up old hats from their bags and putting them on. It was very moving.

I knew I was finished. I got one vote for prefect (which was my own) and 230 people signed a petition to get me expelled. And Mr Harrison, the windy fascist, was on the top of the list.

I probably would have been quite disheartened if my personal life hadn't started to really take off at the same time. It was Barry. I was rapt. He was a lot older than me and went to the tech college in Hurstville. He had a beautiful well-formed chest and looked a lot like the man in *Ben Hur* who wins the chariot race. Barry was my sister's boyfriend's best friend and he'd been on my diary list for three years. He hadn't always kept his top position, though, mainly because the chance of winning him seemed so remote. Occasionally, he'd be dropped right down if there was another guy who was actually taking me out. Like boys from the school special or the Fellowship or, more recently, from the Young Liberals. I joined the Young Libs when I'd been through the talent at all the Fellowships and hadn't come up with much. If you went to the Lib meetings you got invited to a lot of parties. I thought this was pretty generous because it was still quite a while before I could even vote for them or anything. They just took you on trust. I tried the Labour Club, too, but they had a much higher ratio of meetings to outings and made you hand out leaflets on Saturdays. With the Libs you didn't need to show any commitment at all.

But I must say my feelings for Barry remained constant through my many changes of religion and politics. I sent him a secret Valentine every year with a poem in it. Well, not completely secret. I used to write my initials in tiny printing somewhere on the page, just to give him a hint. I mean, otherwise, what's the point? Anyway, my last poem must have worked because he finally asked me out.

I wish by every star above, that I could sign my
    name,
But if I did our relationship could never be the
    same.
For my identity you will never know
Until I strike my final blow
A blow which will end my three-year wait
And seal up your misty fate
The secret of my person will be my bait
And I will get you soon or late
Please don't fight it, it's destined to be
Just stay single and wait and see.
I've made up my mind that you will be mine,
I've set my task out on the line.
I will catch you unawares
So beware, dear Barry, beware.

He invited me to John's twenty-first which was only six weeks away and I went on a special diet to lose the fat off my thighs for the big night. It was a new Jewish plan called the Israeli diet and all the girls at school were on it. It was really popular because the Israelis were winning their war against the Arabs at

100

the time. It was a month of apple cores and well-sucked cheese-stick wrappers. Four days cheese, four days apples, then four days cheese again. It was a particularly sickening diet, though, because you had to eat the same sort of cheese for the whole four days. My friend Pam started on some blue vein that her mother had left over from a dinner party and by Day 3 she was rancid.

We wanted to look like the girls in the ads who bounced around the Hawkesbury River on giant inflated Coke tins. They had long blond hair and pelvic bones that stuck out like flagpoles. The test was to lie on your back in a bikini and try to see your pubic hairs. If your stomach sunk in far enough, then the bikini stretched right across the bones and you could see everything. Pam and I spent a lot of time looking down. It was hard for Pam. She was my friend with the jumping hormones and her breasts were so big that she could hardly see past them to her belly button. Let alone anything else.

Anyway, we tried. We'd lie out in the backyard on Saturdays with our transistors on and our legs surrounded by 'sun-catchers' made up of Alfoil and chopsticks. We ate Kraft slices and waited for our stomachs to sink. We'd do everything in the back-yard; pluck eyebrows, shave legs and wear porridge masks to draw the blackheads out. Sometimes the masks didn't work because Sally was always licking them off. Mum said there must have been sugar in the oats.

Saturday afternoons were devoted to getting ready for the party or the harbour cruise or the drive-in. It was really hectic for me with my long wavy hair because I had to roll it on to beer cans to stretch the kink out. It took ages to dry and the weight of the tins was pretty hard going. Things got a lot easier when they started putting KB in aluminium.

By the time John's twenty-first came along, I was almost perfect. Mum made me a special outfit, a pair of formal long culottes in green brocade with a matching top that just reached below my bottom. I was still working at the hairdressers and Tony gave me a free comb-up. The ringlets and curls were so elaborate that it took fifty-nine bobby pins to keep them there. I know because I handed them up. Pam cancelled her own date with Steve to help me get dressed. I took hours because I wanted to be just right.

I know Barry appreciated all the trouble I went to because he commented when he came to pick me up.

'T'riffic.'

He rushed in with his hair still wet and his shaving nicks still bleeding and a crease on his Fletcher Jones trousers that you could cut bread on. His mother always had his clothes pressed ready for him because his Saturdays were hectic too, what with football or sailing or meeting the mob down the pub for a drink.

Mum saw us to the front door with the final words: 'And remember, Moya, you can always *stoop* to pick up nothing.'

Barry didn't take offence! He knew she didn't mean *he* was nothing! She was talking about the sex thing. You know, degrading yourself and getting into trouble. She said it to all her girls on their way out, every time. She'd even said it to Rhonda.

The party at the golf club was a rage of a turn. The club was really beautiful, right on the George's River opposite the airport, and from the balcony you could watch the 727s taking off. The smorgasbord had devon and potato rolls done in a key shape and a band, the Spinning Wheels, was playing. Afterwards we all rolled up to Bexley RSL.

The man on the door wouldn't let me in. He said there was a club rule about women wearing pants. Mum and I hadn't even thought of that! Barry was really furious about it and called the manager to complain. Finally the two of them found a solution. I just had to take the culottes off and wear the top like a dress. Perfect. It was pretty rude because you could see my bottom whenever I lifted my shoulders but apparently there weren't any club rules about that. I just stomped to the music with my arms folded, Barry said I looked good and I was very grateful to the Israelis.

I didn't get home until 3:00 a.m. and Barry kissed me for ages in the car. I never realised there could be so much difference between an eighteen-year-old and a twenty-year-old. Maybe Barry was just old for his age but he was definitely a man and not a boy. I came to the conclusion that all older boys tongue-kiss on the first date. I used to think it was off but not with Barry. It just seemed natural and not rough at all.

We started going out every week and I knew Barry really liked me. Not that he said so, not in so many words. He was a lot like Dad, really. He was a real man's man, which is funny when you think about it.

I mean, there I was trying to change Dad all those years and then I go and fall in love with someone just like him. I could really understand Mum much more after that and the power of silent love. I wrote down every nice thing that Barry ever said to me.

'There's something about you I like. I don't know what.'

'Your legs aren't bad in mini skirts.'

'Give us a kiss.'

We started spending a lot of time pashing in the car in the driveway. Dad turned a blind eye because he liked Barry so much but I could tell Mum was worried. She said she had the same feeling about me and Barry as she had about Rhonda and Bob. I got scared about that but she said not to worry because she trusted me. She said I should just try to imagine she was always sitting in the car with Barry and me and then I'd make the right decision.

But it was really hard to imagine Mum in the back when Barry and I went parking.

We went a lot, mainly to Brighton-le-sands where there were some good places along the beach. The only trouble was it was so popular that sometimes you'd have to drive around and around until somebody pulled out. There were two kinds of parking, ordinary and pet-parking. In the first kind you sat up and with pet-parking you laid down. We laid down the first night we went.

I kept a record of it all in my diary with asterisks to show how far we went. Like one for tongue-kissing, two for breast-touching over the bra, three for breast-touching under the bra and so on. But as the sessions got longer and when we moved into the back seat, there was no room for Mum any more and the number of asterisks just made me guilty.

A girl at school, Brenda, had been having it off with her boyfriend for ages. Not that anyone knew. She was the quiet type, the sort you'd never pick. She just got carried away one night and that was it. Just like that. After that she thought she was pregnant every month and she'd sit in history, pounding her stomach and praying for her periods to come. She wasn't on the Pill because Greg didn't believe in it. He said if a girl was on that she could go off with anyone. Anyway, one month Brenda really was pregnant and Greg did the right thing by her, gave up uni and got married. After the baby was born, he seemed to trust Brenda a lot more because he put her on the Pill straight away.

With Barry, it became harder and harder and one night after a barbecue we nearly went all the way. He said I'd have to get something and I did. I found a doctor in the Pink Pages who lived on the other side of the harbour. I was incredibly nervous but one look at him put me at ease. He was about Dad's age and had pictures of his children all over his desk. There must have been six or seven of them, maybe eight, so obviously he was a real family man. He went to church, too, because there was a crucifix over his desk.

But when I told him what I wanted he turned cold, scribbled out a prescription and saw me to the door. I was humiliated and cried all the way home. I cried in the chemist, too, when I got it filled out and then I threw the lot in a rubbish bin outside Rockdale station.

Barry was really cheesed off and I thought he was going to chuck the relationship, for sure. He said the thing that cut him the most was that I hadn't even saved the repeat. I screwed up my courage and tried again. This time I took Chris and we went to the Family Planning Clinic. It was right opposite the university and the doctors were really nice. They had a fantastic range of contraceptives, something for everyone. It was difficult to choose but finally I went for the Pill again. Chris got some, too, even though she'd never had a boyfriend or anything. I think she felt fat and left out.

The trouble was, they wouldn't give you the prescription without an examination. If Chris hadn't been so keen to stay I would have backed out then, for sure. She didn't seem to mind the idea at all. The doctor strapped my feet into stirrups and used an instrument that looked a lot like Mum's spaghetti tongs. He said I wouldn't lose my virginity or anything but I don't know how that could be true considering what he did. Then he got a long hooked mirror and made me look at all my personal parts. He said it was important that I knew where everything was. He didn't say why. Then he said I had a very pretty labia majora and I should be proud. I got the Pill in the end, three months supply of Norinyl 1.

That night Barry told me he'd got a job in the bank. The next day they sent him to Wagga Wagga. It was a two-year appointment and the Norinyl was pushed to the back of my underwear drawer for quite a while. I promised to write him one love poem and a letter every week. After all that, I was back where I started. Mum, the telly and the sound of steel wool on a six-iron.

It was really lucky that Pam's boyfriend had just given her the big miss because we could at least keep each other company. We started to spend Saturdays differently. There didn't seem much point in covering your face in porridge and bleaching your elbows with lemons just to watch Bill Collins. So we'd go into town instead. We'd meet on DJ's corner, walk around looking at the shops and pay off some laybys at Farmers or Horderns or a new shop from Melbourne called Sportsgirl. We always had a lot of laybys going at once and paid $2.00 a week over a few months. It was a great system except that, by the time you got things out, the season was finished and you were stuck with open-toe wedgies in June. But there were no Bankcards and people didn't go much on credit anyway. It all came under the heading of hire purchase or HP which was almost a dirty word and only used by drunks or deros or deserted de factos. De factos were women who had somehow gone off the rails after moving in with someone without marrying them first. Mum and Dad always said the word in a quiet sort of voice they used for 'cripple' or 'cancer'.

It was incredible that they decided to let me go down to Wagga for a weekend. Jenny, the teller with Barry, was getting married and I was invited as the 'and friend'. Rhonda and Sue were really cheesed about it. They reckoned that Mum would never have

107

let them go off like that. They said I was spoilt.

'I wasn't even allowed to stay at a girlfriend's place until I was married. And what's the point then?'

'You made me get home by eleven and the pictures didn't even get out until half past ten.'

'No wonder she's a precocious brat.'

'You let her get away with murder.'

They didn't. Mum and Dad were just too tired to say 'no' anymore. Twenty-five years of pulling in the reins had left them exhausted and Rhonda's tragedy had showed them that it was useless anyway. It's an ill wind that blows no little sister no good.

I would fly down in a Fokker Friendship. I dug the Norinyl out of the drawer, put a pair of white baby doll pyjamas on layby and wrote furiously in my diary. I decided on a new symbol...an asterisk with a heart around it.

I could barely carry my hand luggage on to the plane. It was filled with bath oils and perfumes and new underwear and make-up and a little Tupperware container of porridge. The wedding was pretty much the same as most I'd been to that year, with one bridesmaid looking just a bit better than the bride and the groom in hired trousers that were just a bit short. Barry squeezed my hand right through the service and was so keen to get me alone that he tried to leave before 'Auld Lang Syne' and the bouquet throwing. I wanted a chance at the flowers so we stayed. I caught the bouquet and Barry caught the garter and Jenny and her new husband took off on the two-day drive to Surfers.

I don't know what I was expecting but the bridal

suite at the Wagga Wagga Koala Motor Inn wasn't it. The first misunderstanding wasn't Barry's fault really. He'd put the bouquet on the dashboard and the lady at the motel just saw it and presumed. I felt like a real fake because she said, as newly-weds, we could have a free breakfast. Including the stewed compote.

The room was like any other except that the bedspread was silver with white horseshoes printed on the padding. Well, not exactly white, more grey. Barry said it was the fluorescents. I said 'probably' and then we didn't say anything at all. It was suddenly very quiet. I suspected my white baby dolls were a big mistake and I didn't know whether to change in the bathroom or right there, in front of him. Barry was pretty cool and just took his pyjamas into the toilet.

We tried and tried. Nothing was happening. In the scramble I snatched a look at Barry's anatomy. I'd never seen it that far from a steering wheel before or with so much light. In fact I'd never seen much anatomy at all, other than on Parka Joe or Mr Shackleton, Chris's father. He used to swim at the pool in old cossies with stretched-out elastic in the legs. You could catch a glimpse of the soft, furry folds between his legs while he was sunbaking. But you could never get a really good look. I certainly couldn't say I had actually seen a full scrotum.

As sensitively as possible I asked Barry if he'd been in an accident. He didn't understand. I pointed to the scrotum. He misunderstood and went to sit in the toilet. It took a lot of talking but I finally got him out.

I explained that I'd only heard of men who had two balls and his scrotum was one. But where was the other? Later, under the flicker of the fluorescent Barry had me. And then, in the morning, he had me again, just as the lady arrived with the compote.

It was all so different from the way I'd imagined. It was all so incredibly disappointing. Not that I let on to Barry! I didn't want to hurt him and I figured it had to get better once I'd got used to it. It was hard for me to take it all in. One scrotum, two balls and a strange man eating compote in his Y-fronts. I thought of Jenny, last night's bride, and wondered how she was feeling this morning. Maybe it was different if you got married first. The lady at the desk gave Barry a wink as we left and asked us to send her a photo. Of what?

I left the Norinyl in a sick bag on the Ansett flight back and at the airport Mum talked to me as if she didn't notice a thing. Apparently nothing had changed and within a few days I could go for ages without thinking about it. But I never put the heart around the asterisk.

Pam pumped me for details so I made some up. For all she knew it was really great. I didn't have to lie much really, just smile and look a bit distant. I don't know why I didn't tell her the truth. I should have. That week she made up with Steve and they did it at her place while her parents were at a prawn night. After that, we didn't talk about sex or anything romantic any more. She just smiled and looked a bit distant and I spent most nights at home with Mum.

110

That wasn't such a bad thing really. I mean, the HSC was coming up and I enjoyed a reprieve from all that touching and pretending. I was so behind in my work that there was a good chance I wouldn't get any first levels at all. I needed them to get to uni. I'd decided to be either a journalist or a lawyer. I thought a journo would be more fun but if I were a lawyer I'd have a brass plate and so get to join Miss Pickwright's club. It was a difficult choice and I knew I'd have to work flat out. And Barry was still taking up so much of my thinking time because he always expected a weekly love poem, even after Wagga. Meanwhile, the rich girls had forged ahead and were virtually teaching themselves. Just like in history — I was still sitting under the car with Hitler and Mr Harrison while they'd moved on to the bunker with Eva Braun. Rich girls don't need to spend much time on their boyfriends. I don't know why.

So I was catching up on my notes and pumping out Barry's weekly verse as well as writing special speeches for the school functions. Sarah Adams, the new captain, had turned out to be a dud in this respect. She got so nervous when she had to speak that she came out in red blotches all over her body. They were really obvious, too, because her skin was so white. This was bad publicity for the school and Miss Pickwright knew it. So, whenever a visitor came, Sarah would welcome them in assembly and then I'd get up and tell a few jokes and give the speech. Then Miss Pickwright would have afternoon tea in her office and the prefects would serve the food and Sarah would stand in a corner with her blotches and I'd sit out in the playground by myself. And I never got a badge, not one.

It was very disheartening and quite lonely and I was at my most vulnerable point when I met Stewart just before the final exams. He was so different from Barry. For a start he was twenty-five, a real estate agent and he believed in waiting until you got married. This was a real bonus.

Dad didn't like him one little bit. I think he thought the family was being untrue to Barry by letting Stewart watch the television with us. He also thought there 'must be some bloody thing wrong with him' if he was so interested in 'a bloody kid'. The kid was me. Mum liked Stewart a lot. He was a real smooth talker and brought Mum flowers and special liqueurs and talked to her as if he were really interested in what she said. He sent me perfume and roses and took me to dinner at the Summit revolving restaurant. He'd pay the band to play the theme from *Love Story* as we walked out of the lift and he'd get the roving photographer to take our photo. He drove a special Falcon with noninclusive extras and wore driving gloves of soft leather with special holes for his knuckles. His fiancée had just dumped him a couple of months before. It was hard to imagine why. I was swept off my feet.

I tried to explain to Barry what was happening. I sent him photocopies of Stewart's letters so he'd have an idea of how difficult my choice was. I sent him some of the photos taken at the Summit. I guess I didn't want it to finish with Barry but it did. He wrote and said not to worry because he was sleeping with Jenny now anyway. He said they'd been having sex for ages and her marriage was on the rocks.

So, after all that, I didn't have any choice but to move on to Stewart. There were more flowers and photos and dinners in expensive restaurants. A real courtship, Mum said. It was high romance and no demands at the end of the night. Perfect. And then, one evening, outside the Cabaret Espana, he held me against a wall in the lane and pulled something out of his trousers. It was a diamond. The pay-off had begun.

7

The Awakening

'My beautiful, wonderful gels. The little tadpoles of
1966 are now the frogs of 1971. They have strong legs
and will jump far and high and we will be proud.'

Miss Pickwright's address at the sixth form farewell was really moving. Particularly the bit about the
legs. She was having so much trouble with her own
that this would be her last year at St George as well.
Her arthritis had buckled her back and made her legs
as bowed as an old cowboy's. We hardly ever saw her
in those last months. She stayed in her office with the
gas heater on and made all the necessary announce-
ments from the microphone beside her tea tray. She
was in a lot of pain but she still went to the trouble to
give her gels a beautiful send-off. That's just the sort
of woman she was.

It was really emotional. The fifth formers were
lined up in a guard of honour as we entered the hall.
They sang the school song and crossed their panama
hats above our heads, like in the army. It was incred-

ible and every girl in the school was crying before the ceremony even got started.

Well, almost every girl. My friend Pam wasn't. She said she couldn't wait to get out of the place. She was feeling pretty crappy during the ceremony because she was in a lot of pain from the dog bite. She'd got it at the farewell dance the night before. It wasn't the dog's fault, though. He was trained to do that by the security guards. Miss Pickwright hired them for every dance. She hired searchlights, too. It was to stop kids leaving the hall to pash in the dark corners of the quadrangle. Anyway, Pam went out in the last set with some guy she hardly even knew and the dog found them and got excited and bit her on the leg. The guy got off without a scratch which was pretty unfair. Especially as he was the one who suggested it in the first place.

I wasn't crying, either. I had to hold myself together to give the captain's farewell speech. I said so many nice things about Miss Pickwright that I'm sure she felt really bad about never awarding me a badge. It went off really well and Sarah, the captain, got a terrific round of applause when I sat down. I'd never written Sarah a better speech.

> First comes love, then comes marriage.
> Here comes Moya with a baby carriage.

We wrote little verses to each other in our autograph books. All the kids in Australia signed autographs on the last day but only the single-sex schools used books. At the rough co-ed ones, they wrote all

116

over each other's clothes and bodies. The idea was to destroy your uniform completely as a symbol of freedom. The girls at St George didn't do that. Firstly, we wanted to keep them intact for our daughters and, secondly, Miss Pickwright wouldn't let us. She made us wear them right through the exams too.

I vomited before every paper. Mum said it was nerves but her breakfasts didn't help. She said I needed to keep up my strength and made me eat porridge and eggs and bacon and bubble and squeak. And toast and juice and tea. I barely had time to eat and to vomit before the morning sessions began.

They started off very quietly, the head supervisor saw to that. He was always very strict. He'd spread the lady supervisors around the room to keep a good watch and make them walk back and forth on their toes. They'd give you a really dirty look if you moved your chair or sucked too loud on your barley sugar. They were really old and you could tell they had no idea of what we were going through. They just wanted a day out.

But after about an hour they'd get bored and clomp about and whisper jokes and gather around the man to drink tea. He enjoyed the attention so much that sometimes he'd even forget to change the time on the blackboard clock. Fortunately, Stewart had lent me his special divers watch which he said worked 200 feet underwater. He said it was really expensive and was used by the CIA. He said it was the only one of its kind in Australia. I laid it out on the desk beside a photo of Mum and Dad, an old picture of Barry, a new photo of Stewart, a troll doll, a green kiwi charm and a plastic four-leaf clover that I'd got from the Easter Show. Beverly Trudeau said the clover was useless superstition. She said that if you'd done enough work you didn't need luck and if you hadn't, then luck wouldn't do you any good anyway. In the modern history paper the first question was to give a detailed account of the day Hitler hid under the car. Eva Braun didn't get a mention and the next day Julie brought a rabbit's foot to maths.

Then suddenly it was all over and we just had to wait for the results. The long summer holidays spread before me like a dream and I could do anything I liked. First, I cleaned out my drawers. I graded the contents in relation to where they appeared on my body. For example, panties and bras on the bottom level, blouses in the middle and scarves, jewellery and perfume on the top. Then I catalogued my bookshelf according to the Dewey system and washed and de-fleed the dog. I caught up with *Days of Our Lives* and ate fresh bread for lunch. It was amazing how much there was to do. But, by the end of the first week, I'd done it.

The Slick Chick Employment Agency got me a summer job in a solicitor's office. He was a young lawyer called Henry Rosenberg who had a little city practice specialising in quickie divorces. Henry was small himself and a bit fat with short legs but he was quite sexy in a way. He had those eyes that undress you. He took me on as a temp typist which was good considering I couldn't type. There were just the two

118

of us and he was pretty patient about all my mistakes. Like when I got thrown out of court.

Henry said it wasn't my fault and he probably would have lost the case anyway. But I felt bad about it. The problem was I had to deliver these urgent papers. I'd never seen a courtroom before, except on TV, and I was very nervous. Also, it was unfortunate that I was wearing my new clogs and hot pants. The clogs were beautiful platform ones with wooden soles but they made a lot of noise on the floorboards. I waved to Henry as I ran down the front and the judge stopped talking and eyed me off and then banged his hammer. Just like that. He said my hot pants were disrespectful and my clogs were so loud they constituted a contempt of court. And apparently you're not supposed to wave. He was a cranky old man called Mr Justice Haxton. I thought he was pretty old-fashioned but I liked his name. You know, being called Justice and then turning out to be a judge. The doctor who cut out Mum's bunions was like that. He was Dr Bones.

Anyway, I tried hard for Henry and taught myself to type. I wasn't very fast but then Christmas time is always slow for divorces, people being reluctant to spoil their kids' holidays by taking off. Henry said the applications really flooded in around February after couples had spent two weeks off work together. It gave them plenty of time to realise how much they disliked each other.

Henry was pretty sophisticated really and liked to shock me because I still called a deadhead 'a big Richard' and not 'a big Dick'. These were the days of co-respondents and adultery and Henry's files made *Number 96* look tame. I loved reading them secretly while he was out but I hated the way he read the details into my dictation machine...

'And then he said to me..."You're an asshole, Sheila, a greedy asshole. I'm fucking off." Did you get that, Moya? He said "fucking, fucking". That's f-u-c...'

There was a lot of sexual tension in that office and when I'd describe it to Stewart he'd get jealous. I tried to explain that it was the nature of my work but he'd just clam up and grip the steering wheel until his knuckles turned white.

He wanted me to give up the job and was becoming very demanding in other ways. Like, he wouldn't leave me alone. He was always dropping in at home and expecting me to kiss him. Even first thing in the morning. Kissing Stewart was something you had to psych yourself up for. Sometimes it could take all day. Also, there was the added pressure of him wanting to settle on a date for our wedding.

'He's a creep. I wouldn't trust him as far as I could throw him.'

'He just wants to trap you before you start uni.'

Rhonda and Sue were talking to me again. It had taken seven years and now they were right behind me, stabbing Stewart in the back. His marriage offer had shot me into the limelight. It was the first experience I ever had that the family could relate to. Dad turned down the TV and was very firm.

'I'm telling you, Moya, there's something wrong with him. He's probably a bloody poof.'

Mum was starting to worry, too. She knew she'd encouraged me. Stewart had swept her off her feet as well.

'Maybe you should listen to your father. It takes a man to know a man.'

I was going off him anyway. As I said, he was all over me and I also hated the way he dressed. He had an enormous wardrobe full of really ugly clothes. He shopped at a place advertised on television. If you bought one suit then you got two free *plus, as a very special offer*, a sports jacket, casual trousers and three shirts, two ties, four pairs of socks and a belt. You got shoes as well if you paid in cash and Stewart always did. I tried to tell him that just because they gave him stuff, it didn't mean he had to wear it. There was no binding contract between the parties. It wasn't a condition of sale or anything. But whenever I used legal words, he'd get angry and tense up and grind his teeth together until they screeched like fingernails on a blackboard. I'd get frightened and cry and as soon as I did, he'd stop grinding and apologise. After a while I'd cry, even before he started grinding, just to give myself a break.

Basically, it was all to do with Henry, although Stewart wouldn't admit it. Like the fight we had after I'd worn his diver's watch in the bath. The glass had filled with water and Stewart went off his brain and blamed me.

'Look Stew, you said the CIA had them. They must take baths.'

'Don't give me that. They know only to use them

121

at great depth, under pressure, in salt water.'

That's another thing about Stewart, he was a liar. The watch was obviously just some cheap Japanese job.

'I'll talk to Henry. He'll know what we can do.'

'What would he know?'

'He knows a lot. *Caveat emptor. Ipso facto.*'

'Wake up to yourself. You like him.'

That threw me but I stood my ground.

'You're pathetic, Stewart.'

'He wants to have sex with you. Admit it.'

'I'm finished with you, Stew.'

'And you want it with him.'

'That's it. It's over.'

And I meant it.

His teeth ground and screeched. I stuck my fingers in my ears and started to whistle. Then he tensed up and shook all over and gripped the steering wheel so tight that his knuckles grew and went white and broke the stitching around the little holes in his gloves. This freaked me a bit but I still didn't cry, so Stewart did. I'd never seen a man cry before, except for Victor Mature. It was terrible, but it was finished.

Mum and and Dad were really supportive. Dad said, 'There's as good a fish in the sea as ever came out of it.' Mum said, 'I know what will cheer you up. Guess who's on tonight? Fred and Ginger. *Putting on your Top Hat*! You can help me polish my clubs!'

Just like old times. Fred and Ginger were a bit of a ritual really and rituals are comforting when your life is in ruins. I don't mean rituals like the Aborigines have or anything like that. I mean, just little ways of doing things that sort of seep into you without you knowing it. Like planning the whole year around four words... 'before Christmas' and 'after Easter' or getting the washing up 'out of the way, over and done with and that'll be that'. Cleaning up was one of life's constants. Mum always shot up as soon as tea was over. Sometimes even before. If you ate too slowly you'd have to finish eating at the sink with Mum waiting to let the water out and wipe down. She loved wiping down. The invention of Laminex had done that to women. They couldn't keep their hands off it.

Another ritual was the family party. There was some mysterious common knowledge about the precise moment to lay out the smorgasbord and pop the Star Wine. The first time our dining room table was fully extended and covered in lace and chicken wings, just for me, was the day I got my Higher School Certificate results. Matriculation success for a Bexley girl rated as a sort of Anglican female Bar Mitzvah.

Henry understood about celebrations too. That day he took me out to lunch. We smoked Black Russians and drank white wine, and back at the office he held me against the photostat machine and started doing a lot of things I'd read about in the files. But I stopped him before his wife could have a case against us.

By the time I'd caught the train back to Rockdale I was really sick and just made it through the ticket box to vomit in the litter bin. And then I got home and just made it through the surprise smorgasbord to vomit after the sherry jelly parfait. Everyone took my early exit pretty well, agreeing with Mum when she put it down to 'nerves, just like in the exams'. She brought me in a big plate of cheesecake and the celebrations continued without me. They gathered around the pianola and sang all the old medleys off by heart and had a great night. It was the first time in our family's history that a girl had succeeded at anything. They were so proud, especially my father.

'She's done bloody well. I'll have to give her that.'

Still and all, he was dead set against my plans to do an arts/law degree.

'You can get this bloody law idea out of your head right now. It'll make you as hard as nails.'

He said you couldn't expect to have a profession and get married as well. Dad knew one lady lawyer and she was an old maid. Our family doctor was a woman and she wasn't married either, so that was that. I buckled under the statistics and decided to be a journalist instead. The next day Dad took me to lunch.

Not to celebrate. He wanted to show me newspaper life as it really was. We went to a crowded city pub. It was full of smoke and noise and women in suits drinking beer at the bar. Dad said these women were journos and 'rough as guts'. They looked it, too. They all had loud voices and told jokes to the men and smoked like chimneys. They also looked very, very intelligent.

'Just like blokes. Gotta be. Not their fault, hard life. Probably lezos.'

Lezos? I rushed home and told Mum I was happy to be a teacher. She was so pleased.

'You can always go back to it. Teaching is lovely for a girl.'

I enrolled in arts at Sydney University and waited to learn something lovely.

Orientation. The student paper *Honi Soit* was full of swear words and boys baring their bottoms on the front lawn. I was only reading it so people wouldn't think I was new and feel sorry for me. Also it took my mind off my bladder while I was waiting for Chris Shackleton to arrive. I was dying to use the toilet but there was no way I was going in there by myself. It was unisex! There was one cubicle out of sight of the urinal but that was a disabled one and I didn't know whether you were allowed to use it if you didn't have a wheelchair. Anyway, it just didn't feel right considering healthy people have so many advantages to start with.

So I wriggled my toes, read the paper and sneaked a look at all the goings-on. There was so much to take in. The front lawn looked like a school fête with little stalls sitting side by side, representing the various clubs.

'Destroy American Imperialism. Join the Communist Party.'

They had parties every Saturday.

'Save the Baby Seals. Wine and Cheese Nights Friday at the Old Union.'

There were barbecues with the Existentialists, cabarets with the Choral Society and slide nights with the Bushwalkers. So much was happening and with all my Fellowship experience I knew I would fit right in. I was so excited.

And then, waiting for Chris, I started to realise that the other freshers were very different from me. They were hip. Particularly the girls. They were all tall and slim and very rich-looking. They had long thin fingers with manicured nails and gold rings. I mean, these girls were really hip. They were not St George rich. This was another scene altogether.

The hip girls knew a lot of other students, even on the first day. They were from private schools on the North Shore and uni was full of them. They spoke in light, airy voices with posh accents and looked very relaxed in flared Merivale jeans and white T-shirts with seamless bras. I felt stupid in my yellow tent-dress and cork platforms. I looked just like I came from Bexley. Not that it mattered much. These people wouldn't even know where Bexley was. And not one person I spoke to had ever even heard of St George.

And then I saw Chris. She was pushing her way through a huddle of hip girls in front of the Medical Society stall and looked ridiculous in her huge orange tent-dress and big wooden platform sandals. She was wearing a sun hat and had zinc cream on her nose. I looked at her and then at the hip girls and then at Chris again. And then I made a decision. I pushed my way into the crowd and disappeared before she could reach me. I had her calling my name but I was resolute. I never looked back.

I had a lot of trouble settling in. For a start I'd chosen all the wrong subjects. I was doing English and two histories while the hip girls did subjects like anthropology and philosophy and fine arts. These

126

subjects didn't do you any good if you wanted to get a job but that didn't seem to matter if you were hip.

I met Trevor in a lunch queue. He was stuffing egg and lettuce sandwiches into his pockets and chocolate milk down his shirt and got away without paying for anything. Trevor was a freshman studying arts/law. He was short with pale skin and blond hair that was thinning at the front. The slight balding revealed a high forehead and made him look very intelligent. He lived on the North Shore but had gone to a public school, just like mine. He knew where Bexley was without actually living there himself. He was perfect. He asked me out to dinner and I said yes and that night he came to pick me up.

Trevor was only eighteen but he was quite groovy already. He was wearing wide jeans and sandshoes and had a zodiac pendant around his neck. I knew it, a Capricorn! I felt pretty stupid in my maxi dress and knee-high white boots. Well, they weren't real boots, more like long vinyl socks that looked like boots when you tucked them into shoes. Anyway, I was overdressed and taller than him and the evening was a disaster from the word go.

Mum saw us to the front door and we both waited for Trevor to open it. Trevor waited too. He told me later that he thought there must have been some sort of time lock on it. Then, Mum said her old line about me not stooping to pick up nothing and Trevor took offence and started defending himself. He was pretty convincing because he was studying the theory of nothingness in philosophy. He said Mum couldn't even be certain that nothing existed at all. He said it was a nonargument. Mum became confused and Dad called out that the John Wayne movie was starting and so we left. His friends were waiting outside in the car.

Their names were Paul and Jane and they had wild afros, silver jewellery and unisex jeans. It was hard to tell them apart but by the time we reached the restaurant I'd worked out that Paul was the one with the earring.

The restaurant was a wine bar called Sorens where you could crack your own peanuts and throw the shells on to the floor. I thought it was a pretty untidy way to eat but quite liberating in its own way. We drank vermouth and coke and the others swore a lot and said 'fuck' and 'piss'. It was amazing.

When I got home I told Mum that uni boys had no respect for women because they swore in front of them. I said I wouldn't be going out with Trevor again and she was pleased about that. She said with him around she'd be frightened to open her mouth. The next week Trevor took me to a play.

I spent my scholarship cheque and book allowance on a pair of flared Merivale jeans and a set of long nails. The nails were the plastic ones that you filed yourself. My sister Sue filed mine but I should have got Rhonda to do it. That night, in the darkness of the Old Tote Theatre, I stroked Trevor's hand all through Act 1. I thought it would feel sexy. When the lights came up he had blood all over him and his hands were scratched to pieces. Sue hadn't smoothed the edges! But despite the pain, Trevor hadn't taken his hand away. It was love.

Over the next few months I realised that uni was a

lot like school except you could kiss a lot and drink coffee whenever you wanted. I had my ears pierced and started smoking Alpines and went to films with subtitles. And then I felt ready to join the university drama group—SUDS.

It was a lunchtime pre-production meeting. The room was full of smoke, anaemic faces and black polo-neck jumpers. My unironed jeans were not enough; I still looked too clean and nice and family-fed. Mum would have said the SUDS crowd all need-ed 'a good feed' and Dad would have called them 'bloody poofs and university long-hairs'. And, in a way, I thought that too.

No one spoke to me and I didn't know how to speak to them. Their voices put me off. It was like listening to the members of a camp royal family. I had no chance of getting a part but I auditioned anyway so I could go to the party that night. It was held in a Glebe terrace owned by a lecturer and his wife.

The lecturer was really handsome and very groovy. He was my tutor in English poetry and all the girls in that tute arrived early to be sure of a good seat. He spoke with an English accent and wore safari suits and had his own coffee percolator going all the time. His wife was like most of the wives I'd met around campus. She had long Indian dresses, no make-up and wore her brown hair pulled so tight into a bun that it stretched the skin around her eyes and made her look a bit Asian. She was doing a post-grad degree in matriarchal civilisations and was right into macramé.

She'd made all the hanging baskets that swung from

the ceiling in their house. They hit you on the head every time you stood up. Usually they held plants, I think, but for the party she'd put big plates of food in them instead. It was foreign stuff from the Middle East that I'd never seen before. 'Highway 61 Revisited' was on the stereo, bowls of chopped parsley swayed overhead and everyone sat around the floor, drinking flagons of red wine and looking intense and incredibly intelligent.

No one spoke to me and I spent a lot of time rearranging the shape of my bean bag and lighting new cigarettes. The group beside me were talking films but they obviously didn't get to the movies very much because they only discussed really old shows from the 1930s and the 1940s. They seemed terribly excited about them, though. In fact everyone in the room was talking very loudly, except for the couple in the corner.

It was hard to make out very much because their bodies were sort of smothering each other. The girl was the third-year student who'd just got the lead in the new play. She was celebrating. Suddenly there was a flash of a white breast and the eye of a large, pink nipple staring out at me. Just as quickly it was gone again, disappearing into the guy's mouth. From what I could see he looked pretty old but quite handsome. And then I recognised him. My tutor! His talk on Blake's *Songs of Innocence* had been really inspiring and now here he was with this...breast. The next week he lectured on *Songs of Experience*.

By the end of the night I'd made quite a hit with the film group. They said I was fantastic and a 'trivia head'. They asked me a lot of questions about the old movies and then got incredibly excited when I gave the answers. All those hours in front of the telly were finally coming in handy. I only had to say 'Boys Town' or 'Spencer Tracy' and they'd clap their hands and shriek and roll about on the floor. They were obviously on drugs or something. I left them laughing hysterically after a perfect rendition of the *Robin Hood* theme and I never went to another SUDS party again. I mean, if that was the level of the conversation, I might as well stay home with Mum and Dad.

And that was the last thing I wanted to do. For a start, we were always fighting. I couldn't voice my opinions on anything without Dad picking on me.

'So, that's what they teach you at your bloody university, is it? Bloody lovely, that is.'

I couldn't work it out. Dad was always putting me down and yet he told all his friends about 'my youngest, going to the university'. Mum said he was proud of me but didn't show it. Maybe it was because he was getting sick. It was his heart. He was having trouble with it and had to give up the fags and the grog. He did, too, just like that. He was scared of dying so I gave him a book on reincarnation and tried to tell him about building up good kharma. He said I'd be on drugs next, just like all my university poofter friends. He said the Alpines were just the beginning and I'd turn out to be a communist.

So what are you supposed to say to that? Dad and I were miles apart; he didn't understand anything. Everyone knew the Marxists were radical weirdos and anyway, they held *lousy* parties!

E I G H T

Bexley Flies Out

'So then like, late at night, I take the ceramic turds and put them on some rich person's lawn. Some really manicured lawn, right? And then I wait in the bushes until the morning when the owner comes out to pick up his paper and I watch his face as he sees the shit, right? He goes ape. It's fantastic.'

Nick the Turd was one of the members of our group. He was a fine arts/law potter who drew a lot of his inspiration from animal faeces. He made these dog turds and then took them into rich suburbs to shock the residents. They were very good turds, too, very life-like. He said he wanted to put a sense of humour back into art and take it to where the people were. Nick was an anarchist and was only studying law to please his parents.

Then there were Trevor, Geoffrey, Anoushka and Greg. Greg was going to be really rich as soon as his grandfather died, Anoushka would be rich when her father died and Geoffrey was rich already. It was a terrific group and it never mattered to them that I was a Bexley girl. They were really natural and just acted as if I were born on the North Shore too.

But I wasn't and I knew it. I wanted to learn how to do things properly. I picked up a lot just by visiting other people's homes, especially Trevor's.

His mother, Mrs Beattie, was a lovely lady whose family had always been well-off. She wore stockings and high heels all the time, even in the house. She had her hair set every Friday and a comb-up every Tuesday. She put flowers in the toilet and doilies under all the vases and sent 'thank you' notes on personal paper after she'd been out to dinner. David Jones delivered parcels COD to her house. She used special scissors to cut up roast chickens and put cloth napkins on the table. The Beatties ate dinner quite late, sometimes not before eight o'clock.

Our family always ate early. I don't know why. Maybe to get cleared up before the good things started on the telly. The Beatties hardly watched TV at all. They never put their pyjamas on until they were going to bed, either. In Bexley, getting changed for dinner meant being in your nightie and dressing-gown and sitting up at the table by six o'clock.

I studied hard at uni, mainly because I was petrified of being found out. I thought I'd probably slipped through the net by getting there in the first place and I needed to do extra well to avoid detection. The hip kids didn't have this problem. They regarded university as their birthright and just did whatever they liked.

I researched my essays in the post-graduate section

of the library, called Stack. It was also the only area that had a smoking section. They had lots of old literary journals there and you could find ideas that nobody else had. I got a distinction for a *Troilus and Cressida* essay that I based on a 1932 thesis by Johnathon R. Willis Jnr of the University of Wisconsin.

It was important to have slightly original ideas if you wanted to get high marks. I learnt this by watching my old school captain, Sarah Adams. Sarah was doing brilliantly at uni but you'd never know it from her performance in the tutes. She never said a thing. Nothing. At first I thought it was because of her nervous rash but then I realised she was saving all her best theories for herself. She didn't want other people picking them up and using them in the exams. I tried to do the same but I'd get so excited if I came up with a good idea that I had to tell everybody. In any case I was never *really* convinced that I had anything worth pinching and I thought it was important that the tutor knew I was trying. As it turned out, he knew Sarah was trying because they met for private discussions after class. He was the professor who sucked the breast at the SUDS party. Not that I think he was doing that to her. Sarah was bright enough to be allowed to keep her ideas and her breasts to herself. And she probably did.

My uni group thought kids like Sarah were dickheads. I loved them for that. We'd all meet in the Manning Building to drink coffee and talk for hours about life, art, Aborigines, television, everything. They were studying law with Trevor and were really his friends to begin with. Trevor didn't go much on my old friends.

Like Chris. I'd see her walking around campus sometimes but we didn't have much to say to each other any more. She'd gone right off after getting involved with a married man. He was a bus driver she'd met while she was working as a conductress during the holidays. She rode around on the 472 or the 491 so she could see him on his breaks. They had sex on Friday nights while the bus waited outside the trots for the races to finish. They did it in the dark, upstairs in the back. Sometimes they'd do it in the middle of the day, too. He'd finish a run and drive the bus down to Bondi to park by the beach with SPECIAL up on the destination board. Chris wrote most of her essays on the Rockdale-to-Drummoyne run but she still got distinctions. She was well on her way to double honours.

Sometimes I felt guilty and thought about inviting her out with us but I never did. Our weekends were so great I didn't want to spoil them by taking more of Bexley to the North Shore than I absolutely had to. It was hard enough believing I belonged there myself! Every Friday we'd go to Geoffrey Freeman's place. Geoffrey's parents were professional people who worked hard all week and then blew out with grog and pills on the weekends. They weren't like real parents at all.

The first time I went there we were listening to *Cocker Happy* at full volume and woke Mr Freeman. He came into the lounge room, completely naked except for a little flannel held in front of his penis.

He asked us to 'turn the fucking music down, please', in a quiet English voice. I couldn't believe it. For a start, you'd never catch my father saying 'fucking' and 'please' together and, secondly, Dad would never go to bed without his pyjamas. Just in case there was a fire or a burglar or something.

All the kids loved the Freemans because they were so liberated. Geoffrey could have girls stay the night and his parents would just get up in the morning and make them breakfast without saying anything. On the weekends, they'd cook big roast dinners that were never ready before midnight because they'd get waylaid telling us stories. Like the exact details behind the conception of each of their children. Susie after a bottle of green Chartreuse in a railway hotel, Geoffrey in a car halfway to Brisbane, Lucy in the baggage compartment of a French train.

They only got really angry once. It was about a month after a big party at their place. I remember the party well because I'd got so drunk that I passed out. Everyone was scared and got Mr Freeman out of bed to have a look. I came to and saw his flannel swaying over me and just before I was going to pass out again he said, 'Now, how would you like a nice piece of greasy bacon sliding up and down your gullet?'

It did the trick. I jumped up and raced into the bathroom to vomit in the toilet. As it turns out the bathroom was actually the laundry and the toilet was actually the catcher attachment of the lawn mower. But I still felt a lot better. Anyway, for weeks after that there was a terrible stench in the house and no one could find where it was coming from. I knew it wasn't the mower, though, because I'd hosed it out straight away.

When Mrs Freeman finally found the smell she went right off her head. Apparently, someone had gone into the linen press, done a big turd and hidden it between the clean sheets. It took that long to find it because the Freemans didn't change their sheets that often. But that wasn't the point. The point was, there was a shit in the cupboard and it wasn't one of the family's. We all knew it was Nick the Turd, of course. He was becoming more anarchic every day and was bypassing the ceramic factor of his work completely. It was a real credit to the Freemans that they offered to pay for some counselling. That's just the sort of people they were.

Not that I could tell Mum and Dad much about the Freemans or anything else. They worried about me 'changing' and wouldn't have understood why I liked all these things. It was hard because I didn't really fit into Bexley any more but I didn't fit in completely with my new friends either. I was sort of landlocked between the suburbs. A social misfit. And then I met Louise who was my 'dream' friend, an Anne of Green Gables of the North Shore.

My parents liked her a lot. She was a very cultured girl who studied medieval history and had a brother who went to a private school. They lived in a suburb that was especially for people who'd made a lot of money recently. Or looked as if they had. My cousin did some babysitting in that area sometimes and she said you wouldn't believe the way some people lived. There'd be a speed-boat in the driveway and beautiful reproduction furniture in the lounge room but nothing to eat in the fridge. It was all for show.

I'm pretty sure Louise wasn't like that, though. She spoke French and wore reading glasses and genuine silk scarves from Italy. She was the first person I ever met who had migraines instead of headaches. She said 'enhunce' not 'enhance' and 'dunce' instead of 'dance' and pretty soon I was talking like that too. Whenever I could remember. Louise was planning to tour Europe for the Christmas holidays and she asked me to go with her. I couldn't believe it. Louise would be the perfect guide to cultural enlightment.

Mum and Dad were really keen on the idea and said they'd pay. They liked the cultural aspect and they thought it might get me away from any 'unsavoury influences', meaning most of my friends. They thought my group was filled with wild, drugged homosexuals. Come to think of it, it was, too. Anyway, the family had a big fight about it because Rhonda and Sue reckoned it was unfair.

'She always gets everything.'

'We never got that.'

'No wonder she's up herself.'

'She's always on to you for something.'

'You bring it on yourselves.'

'It's pathetic.'

It was such a mean scene that Mum got a fair idea of what would happen when she and Dad died and the three of us tried to split up their things. That's when she discovered the adhesive dots.

She bought them in three different colours and stuck one under every valuable thing in the house.

Like a red dot for Rhonda under the porcelain figure of the Shepherd Girl, a yellow dot for Sue behind the Namatjira print and a green dot for me under Nana's old teapot. I could have told her it was useless. Sue and Rhonda changed the dots whenever they felt like it. Rhonda even bought a whole packet of new red dots just for herself. At last count I saw that my inheritance amounted to the Jason recliner, a print of Van Gogh's *Sunflowers*, a chipped crystal vase and the vertical grill. Both Rhonda and Sue had a grill already.

Anyway, after all the fighting Dad said he wouldn't pay for the whole trip, but he would go halves. So I got a job at McDonalds, just across the road. I could lie in bed and see the tip of the giant M through my window. If I looked out the other window, I could read the numbers on the bellies of the new jumbo jets as they flew overhead. It seemed like fate really, sort of destiny under the flightpath.

I was only nineteen but felt really ancient compared to the rest of the staff who were still in high school. It was hard for them because the manager put the oldest workers on the front counter and made the youngest fry the burgers in the back. Most of them had teenage acne to begin with but after a few nights over the greasy skillet their pimples erupted like nothing. They kept nicking chips, too, and getting fat and it ended up like a freak show back there. It was a very unaesthetic work environment, I can tell you. The only thing that kept me reasonably conscientious was the thought of my trip with Louise and...the Hamburger Spies.

140

McDonalds employed people to go around to all their stores and order food and then report on service, quality and cleanliness. They were usually star staff members who had been selected to attend the University of Hamburgerology in America and were waiting to leave. They were generally pretty ugly young guys with close-set eyes, tiny moustaches and body shirts with wide colourful ties. They'd given up their jobs in banks or car yards and were completely brainwashed. They totally believed in the concept of a 100 per cent full beef pattie with a minimum waiting period.

But you couldn't recognise a Hamburger Spy for certain. A lot of people look like that. So you had to go through the McDonalds Seven Steps of Service every time, just in case. I did the whole thing in an American accent to make it more authentic. Every new employee was issued with the Seven Steps printed on a card, for reference.

First you greeted the customer and then you got his order. When he was finished you suggested he buy something else. Then you said it wouldn't be long. Then you smiled as you gave him the change, said he should have a nice day and you'd see him next time. You had to say all this even if the customer was just a young kid. Even a child. At McDonalds it was quite possible that a toddler was on the payroll. You just never knew.

If you got low marks from a spy you got the sack. If you got really high marks the staff would get a prize. I won a digital wall clock for the Staff Relaxation Centre after my first inspection. Apparently, the spy had been really impressed with the accent.

They took the clock away when I complained that the staff would rather have a radio or a ping-pong table or something. I said the clock was a corporation trick to keep the meal breaks short. It always ran five minutes fast. I really stuck my neck out but the other employees didn't appreciate it at all. They gave me the cold shoulder when the clock was removed and really got into me when the plastic gold plaque for Store of the Month was taken down. The next week I was frying burgers out the back and that's where I stayed until I had enough money to fly out.

Everyone turned up at the airport to see us off. My aunties drank shandies with the drugged homosexuals and told them stories about the white slave trade and the thieves in Italy who buzz around on motorbikes and chop off girls' arms to steal their shoulder-bags. My auntie Gloria knew a lot about all that. She'd been on a *Women's Weekly* world tour and said Venice was filthy. She'd been to 'Dreary Lane' and 'Convent Garden' in London, too.

'The memories will last you a lifetime but keep track of your slides, you forget what's what. And prepare yourself for the human digidation. There's lots of that. I'm telling you, if you learn nothing else, you'll come back knowing Australia's the best bloody country in the world.'

The best? And I'd just sold thousands of Big Macs to get out of it?

There were the usual going-away presents. A *My World Trip* diary, a sun hat that folded into an overnight bag and an overnight bag that folded into a map of the best duty free shopping in Singapore. Mum reminded me about stooping to pick up nothing, Dad pressed a $50 note into my hand, Trevor tongue-kissed me in front of both of them and I was off.

We were incredibly excited. It was a student flight on a Qantas 727 and I really appreciated the little extras they gave us. Like the tiny bottles of Blue Grass eau de cologne and the free sanitary napkins in the toilets. I mean, on a student flight you'd think they'd cut down on touches like that. They even had free postcards of the plane to send home.

Actually, it was the postcards that first started me worrying about Louise. As soon as we finished the in-flight meal, she wrote a card about it to her mother. She described everything, right down to the choco-late mints we had with coffee and the way the cutlery came in plastic bags. Maybe she wasn't so sophisti-cated after all. She wrote another card after the in-flight movie. And another two before we'd even landed in London. We posted them from Piccadilly Circus the minute we arrived.

Louise was our navigator and she tried quite hard. Any problems we had were due to the fact that she couldn't see much without her glasses. She wouldn't wear them because she said they made her look daggy. They did, too. But that wasn't the point. The point was that she'd taken on the job and then she couldn't read the maps.

She couldn't see properly in the art galleries either and that was really silly because she was right into art. She knew a lot about it and had decided to concentrate on pre-Renaissance religious painting. She taught me about blue signifying omniscience and ochre lending compassion but I got sick of it pretty quickly. I mean, how can you take someone seriously when they stare at a painting for hours and then turn around and walk straight into a pole? So I'd head for the post-moderns and leave Louise to feel her way around the walls of cherubim. We'd meet in the cafeterias for lunch.

We travelled all over Europe on a Eurail pass which meant you could see as many countries as you wanted for a fixed sum. We spent a lot of time in trains and stayed in youth hostels where we met many interesting people. One guy from Britain was on a 25,000-mile world bicycle tour. Well, that's what it said on his T-shirt. Actually, he'd started the tour twelve months before and had only done ten miles before his bike was crushed under a semitrailer outside Dover. He was saving up for another one and was just taking trains in the meantime.

Then there were George and Merryl who had left New Zealand the day after they got married. They didn't have enough money to stay in hotels, though, so they'd spent their honeymoon in single-sex dorms. In twelve weeks they'd had just two nights together! We met them in Amsterdam and went to the red light district to see a sex show. There were lesbians and dog acts and threesomes and a black man with an enormous penis but it still became boring after a while. We would have left after the first session if Merryl hadn't been so keen on another look at the Negro. George couldn't get her out. Two nights in twelve weeks just hadn't been enough.

And then there were the Australians.

'Geez, you wouldn't have anything for the runs, would ya? It's just pouring out of me.'

Brisbane Sue had travelled overland from India and when we met her in the French café she looked really sick. All blown up, like a cane toad. She heaved her backpack against the bar. It was the size and shape of a rolled double mattress and featured a hand-painted jar of Vegemite on the top. She must have heard our English because she sat down beside us with her boyfriend Dave. He was a big muscular bloke from Perth with legs covered in ulcerating coral cuts from southern India. The cuts were the ultimate in surfie souvenirs and Dave constantly checked their condition while we waited for our food. Then he started up a conversation with the attractive Frenchman at the next table. The man spoke perfect English but he did have a strong accent. Dave shouted loud and slow in response, as if he were dealing with a retarded five-year-old.

'Australia? Compared to here? Well, in Australia, the average man can work, say, for six weeks and earn enough for a ticket to Europe. In your country, the man must work, say, fifty weeks, to go to Australia. And *that's* if they let him in. We have bloody tough entry requirements...'

It's a pity we didn't have tougher 'requirements' on who we let out.

Meanwhile, Brisbane Sue kept up a running commentary on her health. Or lack of it.

'My guts haven't been the same since Istanbul. You haven't got anything for cold sores, have ya?'

I wasn't feeling too well myself. The waiter had

145

just brought me a giant pig's head braised in mushrooms. Louise ordered me veal escalope but things went wrong in the translation. They usually did. Louise's French had turned out to be a big disappointment. There was no point complaining because it never did any good. She always made out that she'd intended ordering things, like raw mince, all along.

Brisbane Sue tucked into a big fried steak. She'd got the message across by drawing a frying pan on the tablecloth and making mooing sounds at the waiter. She wasn't very civilised but she was eating well.

'Geez, you wouldn't have any Bandaids, would ya? These wog thongs are rubbing the shit out of my toes.'

Louise said she didn't and that wasn't true. The Parisian chemist had sold her a whole box the day before when she'd ordered my tampons. I was just about to mention them when the manager's dog let out a yelp and a squeal and flew from under our table, into the air and out the door. He was a bull terrier whose stomach had unfortunately come into contact with Surfie Dave's foot. The manager complained, of course, but Dave wasn't put off. He stood up to set things straight.

'This is a fuckin' restaurant, Froggie. It's for people, not animals!'

He sat down and started picking at a weeping sore on his leg. He squeezed and picked until the pus ran down his ankle and on to the floor. Finally, he could relax.

'Hey Froggie, bring us a beer.'

Louise and I gave each other our 'Australians are

146

disgusting' look and took off. We learnt so much on our travels. I loved speeding along in the trains watching whole civilisations just flashing by the windows. I thought a lot about going home and how rich life would be when I could put my new European values into practice. I made a private commitment never to eat sliced bread again. I would drink wine with every meal and go for promenades after lunch. I bought a silk scarf for Mum and a French beret for Trevor and a little leather handbag for Dad, just like the ones men carry in Italy.

As for Louise, well, people say that you never really know someone before you travel with them and people are right. I soon found out that Louise didn't have much *savoir-faire* at all. She wasn't very discerning, either. We split up in Italy after she had it off with a Pompeii guide. We'd met him in the Sacred Love Room. The Love Room was where the ancient Romans conceived their children. The walls were covered in erotic drawings of giant phalluses and, later that night, Gino the guide showed Louise that his forebears had nothing compared to him. She spent the rest of her trip tasting Italian delights with Gino the Genital Giant and I continued on my own.

In Germany I met up with Art and Rip who were 'two American composers currently living and working in Berlin'. They were both extremely cool and had very rich parents. They had their own American Express cards and could really speak French. They were composing in Europe for a year before going back to the States to study business administration at Harvard. Anyway, the three of us became really close

147

and almost had a *ménage à trois* in Hamburg. Only the thought of Trevor saving himself kept me back.

My parents, my aunties and the wild, drugged homosexuals were waiting at the airport when I flew in. As soon as Mum saw me, she started to cry. They weren't tears of joy though, more of shock. I'd put on so much weight with all that unsliced French bread and lunchtime wine that Mum rushed straight home to the Singer and ran me up some tent-dresses to hide the flab. There was only one thing worse than being young, female and fat in our family and that was being young, female and pregnant. And when Mum first saw me she wasn't sure which one I was.

My 'triumphant homecoming' turned out to be a disaster in more ways than one. My uni friends had changed incredibly. Their trips to Asia had turned them all Balinesque with their brown faces, skinny bodies and white cheesecloth. The guys had their hair cut so short that you could see their scalps through it. This was due to a government regulation in Singapore. The customs officials there met every new jumbo with a pair of hair-clippers in one hand and a printed warning to litterbugs in the other. It seemed a high price to pay for a duty free transistor but the guys didn't care. Everyone was fit and happy and imbued with a new eastern calm.

And me? I looked grotesque with my flabby white European winter body and I soon realised that the new clothes I'd bought so proudly would only make things worse. Even if I *could* fit into them! They marked me as conservative and possibly 'exploitive'. Suddenly Italian 'style' was just an example of corrupt western civilisation. My trip to Europe was seen as pretentious. Why hadn't I visited our Asian neighbours first? The criticisms were endless.

Not even Trevor. I knew something was wrong. He'd been to Asia, too, but the changes in him were deeper than just the haircut. He broke it off with me on Redfern railway station the night after I got back. He said he wanted his freedom because monogamous relationships were repressive and uncreative. Apparently his Balinese sexual adventures were totally amazing and he'd been liberated. I made the old crack about Asian sex not being much good because an hour later you didn't feel like you'd had any. He didn't laugh. He looked me straight in the eyes, meaningfully, and said I shouldn't be sad and that our whole life lay ahead of us. I cried and said I was afraid. He promised we'd always be friends. 'Remember, Moya. Life is a journey...travel it.'

It was pretty obvious that I'd have to buy some batik, light some incense and make my own journey as best I could. I decided to keep my European discoveries to myself. I would continue to learn about 'civilisation' in secret.

I started by visiting the NSW Art Gallery. I had come to love the paintings in Europe, particularly the work of the Flemish school. On my first visit to the gallery, I asked the guard to direct me to the Breugels. He pointed down the stairs, to the left. The Aboriginal Arts section??

'Yeah, love, no worries. You'll find plenty of brolgas there.'

The Bexley girl was home.

The Student Hovel

'You walk out that door and I change the lock. If you come back in, it's as a visitor.'

Dad was dead set against the new idea. My announcement that I would leave home for a mixed flat near the uni sent shock waves through the house. With Rhonda and Sue both married, there'd just been Mum, Dad and me for several years. Just the three of us. It was quite comfortable really and very quiet compared to the old days. No queuing for the toilet or fighting about the washing up. Now there were more than enough chairs in the TV room for everyone. We could 'please ourselves', Mum said, 'eat when we like, answer to no one'. And that was true. But we'd lost something as well. And that was true, even though nobody would admit it. There were no surprises any more. No new Jason recliners or vertical grills. There didn't need to be. We had it all and 'wanted for nothing'. At last I was the only child. It was perfect and I couldn't wait to get out.

I was the last rat to desert the sinking ship and Dad tried hard to persuade me against it.

'Once you go, that's it. There's no coming back. I'm not having you walk all over your mother. You won't treat this place like a bloody hotel.'

It was their biggest shock since Rhonda's tragedy and had much the same effect on their nerves. They started to disappear in front of my eyes. Mum was sewing another tent-dress on the Singer when I told her and she stopped in mid seam and crawled into the Jason recliner. She cried for three days and never did finish the dress. Dad put his foot down and ranted and raved. Then he went out and bought a packet of Rothmans and smoked the lot on the back step. The house went quiet. They couldn't understand where they went wrong.

I had meant to tell them before I went to Europe but I kept putting it off. I suppose I knew what was coming. I'd heard a diluted version three years before when Sue had just hinted at moving out herself. She was crushed into submission in one afternoon and ended up marrying John instead. She said that marriage was the only exit visa Mum and Dad understood. She transformed disgrace into triumph with a flurry of white tulle, black hire cars and gift-wrapped Crockpots. Mum and Dad were happy because she had a good man to look after her. I didn't have anyone. They were frightened and humiliated.

Frightened because the world was full of sex and drugs and probably more sex. And humiliated because I was champing at the bit to get into it. They'd have to tell all their friends, of course. The golf ladies had only recently forgiven her for Rhonda and now they would have to know about me.

I stayed in my room to fight the guilt. This was particularly difficult because it had been redecorated as a surprise while I was away. There were new curtains, a matching bedspread, a white flokati rug on the floor and a painted tile on the door, MOYA SLEEPS HERE. It was the tile that was the killer and I almost buckled under. I don't know what I would have done if Rhonda and Sue hadn't rushed to my defence.

'Let her go. You know what she's like. She's always been selfish.'

'So what's the worst thing that can happen to her? Pregnant? Drugs?'

'She doesn't have to leave home to get into that.'

'She probably smokes dope in her bedroom already.'

'Yeah, and it's easy enough for her to have sex here with you and Dad up at the caravan so much.'

'Yeah, and she probably...'

Thanks Rhonda. Thanks Sue. The drugged nymphomaniac prepared her exit.

All my uni friends were making the flight at the same time. We found two inner-city terraces walking distance apart with tiny windows and big cockroaches. My room had a terrific view over the railway shunting yards and Mum cried when she saw it. I don't know whether it was the stained mattress or the stink of cats on heat that upset her. But I suspect it was the mattress. There's something very frightening about strange beds and yellowing pillows when you're old. Also, Mum was keen on a new soap powder at that time. It removed all marks with soaking and I don't think she'd seen a stain for ages, especially one of unidentified origin on a foreign mattress. She took it as a portent of things to come.

Dad shook his head outside the front gate and refused to come in. He couldn't get over it. The student hovel was only a mile or two from our old place in Richmond Street. He thought my friends were ratbags and he didn't think much of their parents either.

They were all North Shore professionals, of course. While the mothers carried boxes of linen from the cars, the fathers stood about on the verandah, smoking pipes. They talked politics and tax deductions and our move to the hovel. They weren't upset about their kids leaving home at all. Mr Watson said, 'The young people of today are terrific.' Mr Hughes said it would be 'invaluable experience, the type you can't put a price on'. Dad shook his head at the gate and said: 'These kids won't know what's bloody hit 'em!'

As he bundled Mum into the truck, he scratched at his backside and burped out loud. As always, he had the final word.

My room was the smallest in the house, the one nobody wanted. I didn't mind it though because, firstly, Dad wouldn't give me any furniture so I didn't need much space anyway and, secondly, it had the only window with a view. The room was completely empty apart from the stained double mattress on the floor. I could lie there and smell the

154

generations of other students in the old striped carpet and look out the window, across the railway yards and on to the city. There was so much to take in. For $16 a week this was all mine. I was free and anything was possible. I could leave the washing up to drain, read in a bad light and go out in the wind without a singlet. The past was wiped clean. It was a whole new beginning.

I decided to decorate the room in the style of a poor French artist. It would be minimalist and authentic. Just a bottle of red wine on the milk crate beside the mattress and piles of books on the floor. I enjoyed it for two weeks and then Mum phoned to say that she and Dad were having second thoughts. They wanted to help me settle in, after all. They dug deep into their cupboards and came up with boxloads of stuff they didn't want any more. There were green venetian-glass vases, a golf trophy with a clock stuck in one of the balls, a chenille bedspread and Rhonda's old glory box. Within a fortnight the suburbs had chased me right into the shunting yards and my French garret was a Keith Lord showroom timelocked in the 1950s. I couldn't tell them I didn't want all this stuff. How could I? Mum was sticking the MOYA SLEEPS HERE tile on the door and Dad was carrying in the big old TV. It was the first set the family had ever owned and he found a great possie for it, too. It fitted perfectly. Smack bang in front of the window.

I shared the house with Anoushka, Geoffrey and Trevor. Obviously, I had my reservations about living with Trevor. He was his own person now and I knew this would be hard for me to accept. But he was still my best friend. He made it clear from the start that he would be bringing other women home and to avoid any possible misunderstandings about the nature of our new relationship, he wouldn't let me do anything for him that a girlfriend might do. In the first week he was late for a lecture so I ironed his shirt. He said thanks, got a dollar out of his wallet and tipped me. When I cried, he got out another dollar. When I still cried he asked me just how much did I think a pressed shirt was worth. He would have given me whatever I said, too. That was one thing about Trevor. He might have been a bit insensitive but he had lots of money and he didn't mind spending it, either. He was the only member of the household with an independent income and that's how he came by his nickname, 'The Banker'.

He did his room up beautifully in the style of a love den. There were velvet cushions all over the floor, a red silk lampshade, the stereo by the bed and a bottle of port in the bookcase. I knew then that reading in a bad light was not going to be anarchic enough for Trev. He was hoping to inflict much greater abuse on his body than mere eye-strain. He had erotic paintings from the *Kama Sutra* on the wall and a whole range of new flares and body shirts in his wardrobe. Trev was gearing up for the sort of action he'd never had with me. The only thing that still worried him was his hair. It was falling out fast and his weekly visits to the Student Health Service for vitamin injections weren't doing any good. In the mornings, the floor of the shower was covered with hair that had still been on Trev's head the night before. His forehead was getting bigger and bigger every day.

All in all, the new household got off to a good start. There were the usual problems about how much we should contribute to the communal kitty and whether chocolate biscuits and deodorant should be classified as essentials. We cooked from a budget recipe book and ate spaghetti bolognese and tuna casserole and for the first few weeks we were pretty organised.

Then term started and the house became a drop-in centre for most of our friends. The demand for Vegemite toast and tea was enormous and people would turn up with a large loaf of sliced Tip Top and a box of teabags and stay for days. Vegemite is a sort of philosophical brain food. It can fuel conversations about the existence of God or women's rights for up to eighteen hours at a stretch. Occasionally the meetings would end if the toaster blew up or the butter ran out or someone criticised Gough Whitlam.

Gough was incredibly popular. He beamed from old 'It's Time' posters stuck all over the walls. These were the halcyon days of the Labor Government when students didn't demonstrate, they applauded. Conscription had ended and there were arts grants and education subsidies available and money was easy to get, if you knew how. My friend Anoushka did. The day she moved in, she applied for an emergency grant. When Mr Hannon, the man at the uni, asked her what she needed it for she just looked embarrassed and said 'women's things'. Mr Hannon was so horrified he gave her $200 straight away. He knew this could buy a lot of tampons. It didn't, though. It bought a new pair of flared designer jeans, a jumpsuit and a long Indian skirt with an embroidered border.

Once Anoushka's story got out, the Student Centre was filled with heavily menstruating girls crying poor mouth. The administration caught on pretty quickly and replaced Mr Hannon with a Miss Churley who fought the girls off with a carton of Meds 100s in her drawer and a desk calendar marked with the ovulation cycle of every female student in the arts faculty.

The arrival of Miss Churley meant we had lots of sanitary protection but very little money. I was living on a low-scale grant while I fought for the hefty living away from home allowance. Technically you were only eligible for this money if you could prove that living at home was intolerable. The most effective proof for female students was to claim sexual interference from your father. Anoushka did. She signed a statutory declaration accusing her dad of every incestuous perversion imaginable. I don't even know whether some of the acts she described were humanly possible. Miss Churley didn't have my doubts. She increased Anoushka's grant immediately. She also gave her a copy of *The Female Eunuch* and a special invitation to the next party at the Women's Collective. Anoushka sold the book, turned down the invitation and bought a fabulous pair of platform shoes to go with the jeans. After that, Miss Churley's office was full of female students claiming sexual interference of all kinds. Girls who didn't have fathers were citing mothers, brothers and grand-parents. When one girl took out a statutory declaration against the family dachshund Miss Churley was finally a wake-up and closed the loophole. The only avenue left for me was to claim that I could no longer live at home because my parents were clinically insane.

I felt pretty bad about it, of course, but I didn't have much choice. I declared Mum a manic depressive and Dad a schizophrenic paranoid with delusions of grandeur. Miss Churley was cynical enough to send me to the uni psychiatrist for confirmation of my claims.

He was a nice man but very intense. He had a nervous twitch in his eye and seemed to perspire constantly. His hands ran with sweat. He'd wipe them dry very methodically, finger by finger. By the time he'd finished one hand, the other would be dripping again. He had a special cloth bandage wrapped around his fountain pen like the sweatbands tennis players wear in tournaments. It was damp and quite grubby but it seemed to do the job. His name was Julian Winton and he was a Freudian. He didn't get me to retell my dreams, though, which was pretty disappointing. I had a fantastic one all worked out with Dad as a tiger snake and Mum as a human doughnut. Julian's was a question-and-answer approach with him providing both the questions and all the possible answers. The conversation was just like taking an oral multiple-choice examination in a tropical climate.

He'd lean his moist body across the desk to deliver

the question. He tried to appear calm but there was fear in his eyes. Julian was obviously petrified of mental illness. He was a kind man who wanted everyone to be happy and well. You could tell by the way he asked the questions.

'So, Moya. Tell me, how are you feeling? Good?' He would beam and smile and nod his head encouragingly for a 'yes' answer.

'Bad?' He would look sad and turn his mouth down like a circus clown, nodding his head from side to side.

'And your dad? How's he? Good?' Smiles and nods.

'Bad?' Frowns and grimaces, eyes pleading for me to say everything was all right.

Well, we did this for a while until I got bored and started asking him some questions. It was clearly a relief. He talked about his family and his work at length. He was very depressed, he said. It was disheartening work.

'You don't know what it's like to be an analyst. People are so pitiful.'

I offered some advice and took him for coffee. At the end of the meeting he declared me to be sane, my parents to be mad and sent a special letter to Miss Churley recommending the allowance increase, with seven months of retrospective payments. This took the grant back to June 1973, the date I'd claimed Dad first starting thinking he was Adolf Hitler.

It was good to have a little bit of extra cash in the bank. It meant I could take myself out to dinner and this was important. It was hard going sitting in the lounge room all the time, eating tuna casseroles while Trevor entertained some girl in the love den. I couldn't hear very much of what went on but Trev told Geoffrey he was getting into some pretty heavy sex in there. He didn't discuss it with me and that hurt. We'd never had secrets before. I would have told him about my sex, if I was having any. As it was, the closest I came to a male ejaculation was when I opened the refrigerator in the mornings.

Geoffrey had sex in the fridge. Well, sperm in the freezer, anyway. The medical school paid well for semen and Geoffrey would produce heaps. He'd store it in little plastic bottles beside the frozen peas. He took his work very seriously and sometimes he'd promise to supply more than he could come up with so he'd have to get Trevor to help.

Anoushka and I found the semen a bit off-putting. Anoushka was a complex girl. She seemed so confident and sophisticated when it came to getting funds but she drew the line at mixing money and sex. She was a bit of a romantic really. She'd had sex for the first time a few months before. It was on a village ceremonial bed in Bali and she said it was an amazing experience, especially after the omelette! She only wore batik after that and every time someone lit up a clove cigarette she'd get sad and climb into the bean bag with a flagon of sherry. She'd stay there until the sherry was finished or someone else demanded time in the bag.

Technically, the bag belonged to Trevor but it was a kind of embryonic refuge for us all really. That's how Julian would have described it, I guess. For me it was the student equivalent of the Jason recliner. Everyone needs a place to feel secure when life is uncertain. In the hovel there was always so much drama going on that the bag was in demand twenty-four hours a day. It was like a drug and everyone needed their fix.

For example, Geoffrey used it to get over his disappointing love affairs. He'd sit there with his guitar, playing sad ballads and singing them—sort of to himself. No one took much notice. He'd just grab the bag whenever he could, play for a few hours and then leave. Geoffrey never had much luck with girls which was probably why he was so conscientious about those little bottles in the freezer. He was a bit of a sad character really. An only child. His mother bought all his clothes and dressed him like an Australian Donny Osmond, right down to his underpants. You could always tell which jockeys on the line were his. They were the only ones with a koala bear and 'Cuddle me' printed on the pouch.

Geoffrey really wanted to be a folk singer but his family pressured him into medicine. I think his mother and father were a bit disappointed in him really. They didn't value the artist in him at all. His dad made a speech at Geoff's twenty-first which illustrated this perfectly.

'To my son. Fifty per cent sportsman, fifty per cent academic.'

Trevor called out something like 'What about the arts, Mr Hughes?' Mr Hughes was irritated by the interruption but he never missed a beat.

'Oh yes, and a few per cent for the arts...'

With a father like that it was no wonder Geoffrey

162

spent so much time in the bag. He needed it. We all did and this gave Trevor a lot of power in the household.

Trev, the Banker, owned every desirable item in the place. The colour television, the stereo, the sharp bread knife, the cheese board, everything. He usually kept them locked in his love den to impress any girls he might bring home. We all understood that but it still made us feel pathetic. Geoffrey, Anoushka and I would sit outside his door just waiting to be invited in. If there was something really good on the telly or one of us had a new record we wanted to hear then we'd strike a bargain. Trevor rarely had to wash up or put the garbage out or clean his hair from the shower recess. The rest of us did these happily, in exchange for an hour in the bag or a late-night movie. Occasionally one of us would rebel and tell Trev to do his own work but that only meant exile from the den for a good week or two and we were all too desperate for that. The first months in the hovel were exciting, that's for sure. But they were a bit scary and lonely, too. And then came Luke.

'Prithee fair lady, look kindly upon this poor wretch, this pitiful rapscallion, this grotesque and ugly fool.'

But Luke wasn't ugly and he knew it. He was drop-dead gorgeous. I was in the canteen queue and he popped up out of nowhere.

'Fear not maidenhead nor chastity, my sweet maid. I beg not that. Merely a *soupçon* of God's elixir, a trickle of pressed beans from the colonies, a...'

Apparently he wanted a cup of coffee. He flashed a

pair of huge, dangerous eyes deep into mine and said he couldn't wait in the line. He didn't have to. As far as I was concerned this man would never have to wait for anything, ever again. I was in love.

He was an arts/law student majoring in English literature and he spoke entirely in Shakespearean prose. He had holes in his jeans, no shoes, flowing scarves around his neck and chickens in his hair. Not real chickens. Just those little fluffy ones with wire legs that Darrell Lea put on top of their Easter eggs. Luke had masses of black curly hair and he'd thread the chickens in it and walk around the uni as if he were normal. He was very dramatic and recited Keats and Shelley off the top of his head. He'd burst into verse over lunch or on the bus or anywhere.

'In Xanadu did Kubla Khan . . .'

I was so excited that I took him straight home to meet Mum and Dad as a surprise on Mother's Day. I should have got her the jaffle iron instead. Luke was entirely out of place at a backyard barbecue. The family tried hard, though, even Dad.

'Sausages, mate?'

'Thank ye, good sir. Naught compares with a fine pouch of minced swine, a gently roasted phallus, a . . .'

'What about a jacket potato, then?'

'Ah, the king of the earth resplendently robed . . .'

'Jesus Christ, mate, they're getting cold. Is that a bloody "yes" or a bloody "no"?'

'In truth, it is a yes, it is a yea, it is a . . .'

It was a long day that moved from bad to worse. Mum saw us to the door. She signed off as usual.

164

'Remember, Moya, you can always stoop to pick up nothing.'

Luke's eyes opened wide at Mum's poetry. He thought he'd finally met a twin soul.

''Tis true and well said, old mother of maidens. For what treasures hath the girl child when innocence is flown?'

This was too much for Mum. She broke down and cried and told me he was a-fuzzy-haired-freak-on-drugs, a weirdo! I knew all that, of course. That was just what I loved about him! Not that he was on heavy drugs, his eyes just looked as if he was. His eye-liner would run and then scratch his pupils under the contact lenses. That's another thing about Luke. He looked terrific in make-up. He was a real Mick Jagger. But without the lips.

On our third date we went to see *Last Tango in Paris*. I found the sex scenes pretty frightening, especially the one with the butter. Afterwards I got an even bigger shock in Luke's room when I saw a huge tub of Miracle Polyunsaturated Margarine on the bedside table. I was just about to shoot through when he explained. It was to eat with supper, he said. He had it all prepared. There was French bread and wine and cheese and gerkins. He said he could appreciate the misunderstanding, considering the film. There'd been 'that other little upset', too. A used condom had been tacked to his door.

One of his house mates had put it there as a joke. He was a pretty off guy who was nicknamed the Animal because of his reputation with women. Apparently, the size of his penis had something to do with it too. Luke said he had the biggest phallus on campus with a head the size of a Riverland orange. The Animal was always putting condoms on Luke's door. And doing other things as well.

Luke was a smooth operator and his room made Trev's love den look very tame. He had the whole seduction routine right down. He laid the supper out on the bed and I'd barely had time to stab a gerkin before he laid me on the bed as well. He reached down beside him and flicked a switch. The lights went off and the tape-recorder came on. Perfect. It was a Dylan song, 'Lay Lady Lay', and I was ready for anything Luke wanted to do. This was obviously the sort of experience you left home for.

Then suddenly, out of nowhere, the music stopped and other sounds came out of the speakers instead. It was heavy breathing and the screams of a woman climaxing and calling, 'More, more!' There were male grunts and filthy words and then silence. The Animal had been at it again.

I would have left but Luke held me firm. He said we shouldn't reward the Animal by letting him get to us like that. He put on another tape and started to kiss me again. I melted. Then he mumbled something in my ear. I couldn't make it out. We kept kissing. He mumbled again. I thought it was Renaissance love talk. I undid his shirt. He kept saying something over and over but I didn't want to spoil the atmosphere by asking him to speak up. It was obviously important. He moved away from me to speak and I waited for the words of love.

'Thou art protected against bastards?'

Against what?

'The unwanted fruit of my loins.'

Contraception! I shook my head and soon he was kissing me again and fiddling for something in the drawers beside his bed. It was dark but he knew exactly where they were. Apparently, the Animal knew exactly where they were as well. Luke opened the tiny envelope with one hand and displayed the contents triumphantly. A square Handiplast bandaid was inches from my nose. It was the type you put on particularly bad pimples and it was more than I could take. The Animal had won. I picked the gerkins out of my bra and got Luke to take me home. He was angry and humiliated and drove off before I could even say goodbye.

There were giggles and whispers coming from the love den as I turned the key in the lock. A telltale red light crept from under Trev's door. I dragged myself up the stairs and tripped over an empty sherry flagon lying by the bean bag outside Anoushka's room. The quiet moans coming from the toilet suggested that Geoffrey was doing his bit for medical research. I pulled the bean bag into the garret and cried. It was all too hard. Dad was right, I didn't know what had hit me. The Bexley girl just wanted to go home.

But I didn't. I grabbed my toothbrush and ran all the way back to Luke's instead. I found him sitting up in bed wearing old flannelette pyjamas and black-framed reading glasses. His contacts were in a glass of water beside the pile of fluffy chickens. He was eating Vegemite toast and writing a scathing poem to

167

the Animal. It was full of metaphors about cocks that crow and citrus fruit that rots on the branch. It was very good. We had sex and it was terrific. The tide had turned and pretty soon it turned for everyone else as as well.

In that year, 1974, sex took off in a big way. Not long after Luke and I got together, all our friends started getting it together too. They mainly did it to each other and there was so much coming and going between the hovels that it was hard to keep up with who was with who and who was straight and who was gay and who was bi and who was just plain lonely. The hovel shook with the release of all those pent-up hormones and there was jealousy and treachery and lots of heartbreak. It became a minefield of explosive emotion and that's a pretty exhausting way to live.

It was particularly hard on poor Trev. What cruel irony! When sex finally took off for everybody else, Trev was going through a dry patch. The women just stopped coming. Just when he wanted to share the love den with the group, the group didn't want to share it with him. He felt left out and very lonely, especially at night when Anoushka and her lovers banged constantly through the floorboards of her room above his own. Trev tried to explain his torment at the weekly house meeting but Anoushka wasn't sympathetic at all. She just said, 'Life's a journey, Trev, travel it.'

It was cruel and unnecessary and marked the beginning of the end. The hovel experiment expired at the end of the six-month lease and Trev and I went off to form another household at the other end of the city. It would be a whole new beginning and this time we would do better. We would let the good times roll. And they did.

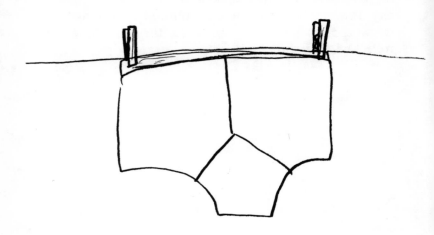

10
Let the Good Times Roll

The new hovel was a great success and survived until the end of our university days. We were a surrogate family, depending on each other for the understanding and support that were in short supply from our real homes. There were Trev, Luke, Howard and me. Trev had a few problems living with Luke at first but he knew that if he wanted me he'd have to take Luke as well. And he did. My father didn't come to the same conclusion.

'You won't walk in here like Lady Muck upsetting your mother. I'm not having you kill her with that bloody drug-addict-poofter mate of yours.'

So Luke was blackbanned. Either I visited alone or I didn't visit at all. And mostly I didn't.

The fourth housemember, Howard, was another friend from the law faculty. He didn't want to be a lawyer, though, he wanted to be a rock star. He filled his room with electric pianos and drum machines and not much else, apart from a few pairs of crusty undies scattered on the floor. He never moved in properly even though he paid the rent every Friday for two years. His mother was a widow and Howie felt bad about telling her he wanted to leave. He used the room as a crash and love until he did.

I was really happy with Luke and he was happy with me. There were a few crises, of course, usually after he'd seduce another girl and then lie about it. The pattern was always the same. We'd have a big fight and he'd pile some clothes in his arms and walk out. Then I'd get frightened and cry and run around the streets looking for him. He was never too hard to find. He'd leave a little trail of dirty socks to where he was sulking in the park or the phone booth or just the backyard. He knew I'd forgive him and I always did. I understood him. Luke was a very complex person. He seemed really wild and eccentric to other people but actually he desperately wanted to be more stable. He just didn't know how and that's why we were so good for each other. I was straight and desperately wanted to be wild. He was crazy and longed to be normal. Perfect. I learnt to say 'fuck' out loud. He hung up his chickens. And Trev had a hair transplant.

It was a new, little-known operation from America. The doctor punched out little sockets of healthy hair from the back of the head and then punched them back in again around the bald bits on the top. It was a simple, trouble-free procedure.

'Help, help, quick, quick...'

It was Trev. I sprang out of bed and ran around in circles looking for a towel before crashing into Luke who was naked too. He was groping along the mantelpiece for his glasses. He never wore his contact lenses any more. For some reason they'd gone the same way as the chickens.

'Quick, quick...'

We ran into Howard at the top of the stairs. It was a frenzy of swaying genitals and bobbing boobs as we hopped around trying to wake up enough to work out what was wrong.

Howie and Luke flew down the stairs and into the street. Maybe someone was trying to get away with Trev's new car. And then I saw the blood. It was everywhere, splattered high along the hallway walls. I followed it to the bathroom and found Trev perched on the toilet, naked and white as a sheet. Blood was pouring from his head. The transplant doctor had punched a hole too close to an artery and it had burst. I pressed my finger hard over the hole and sat down beside him to think.

'Shit, mate!'

Luke was back and the sight of Trev's head had shocked Shakespeare right out of his own.

'Shit, mate!'

Howie was back, too. It hadn't taken them long to work out that the car was not in danger and the cruel jibes from the garbage men about the size of their sleepy members had whipped them back into the house.

Luke said, 'Watch out, Moya. I'll handle it.'

One close look at Trev's head and he panicked. He ran off down the stairs.

Howie screamed at me: 'Cotton wool, quick, Moya.'

'I haven't got any Howard, I...'

173

'Shit, Moya, every woman's got cotton wool!'

He raced off to find a tampon to illustrate his point while Trev and I grabbed some body cover from the linen press and headed for the hospital. I wore a tablecloth and Trev had the new fitted sheet. We passed Luke making his way upstairs with a bucket of soapy water. He was as white as Trev and very disturbed. He said we should go on ahead and he'd give the walls a good clean while we were gone. Howie called from the top window as we got into the car. He'd 'help Luke', he said, 'that'd be best', and waved an unravelled tampon triumphantly as we sped off to casualty.

Luke was still sponging the walls when I got back. He was doing a Lady Macbeth impersonation as he worked, 'Will not all the perfumes of Arabia wash these little walls clean?' and had clearly regained his composure. Trev's head recovered just in time for the final exams. The guys were finishing at the law school and I was sitting for a diploma of education.

Sex with Luke had taken its toll on my academic aspirations long ago and I had given up my honours studies in English to take out an ordinary degree the year before. No one had tried to stop me and it was only when I saw Sarah Adams hard at her thesis in the library that I regretted my decision. She'd gone from strength to strength and was already tipped for a tutorial position next term. You knew just by looking at Sarah that sex would always take a back seat. It always did for girls like that; they were confident enough to go without it for years on end. They just did one thing at a time and did it well. I tried to do everything and it was getting me nowhere. My old schoolfriend, Chris Shackleton, had given up her honours work as well. In fact she was leaving uni all together to have the bus driver's baby. She'd put sex in the back seat, too, in a way. The only difference with Chris was that she'd jumped in after it. She conceived on the slashed vinyl cushions during a SPECIAL run of the 491.

Exam times threw the hovel into panic. There were histrionics and cramming around the clock and sleep was seen as an antisocial activity. If you went to bed then you let the whole team down. The boys held study conferences and visited other student houses with box-loads of books and cartons of cigarettes, staying for days. I did a meals-on-wheels-type service, delivering thermoses of hot tuna casseroles. This cut into my own study time but the boys were really grateful, like soldiers receiving Christmas parcels on the Western Front. Anyway, their work did seem more pressing than mine.

We took caffeine tablets for alertness and special fruit juices for stamina and laid off dope all together. Luke said it was a well-known fact that marijuana reduced the effectiveness of the short-term memory and this was serious. We trusted our futures to the power of the brain's two-day retention cycle, storing away masses of information that we never expected to be available by the end of the week.

This year the law exams proved to be the toughest ever and by the last week things looked grim. There were still two papers to go and the guys knew they had run out of time to cover both. Luke hit on the only solution, a medical post.

A post was an exam students could take in the

holidays if they were ill during the exam period. The only problem was that you needed a doctor's certificate and they were hard to get. Doctors knew all the student tricks, probably because they'd used them themselves. While Howie and Trev continued to study, Luke spent two precious days working his way through the *Reader's Digest Medical Encyclopedia*. Neuralgia.

Apparently, neuralgia had no visible symptoms but involved searing pain with even the slightest movement of the neck. There were no tests to ascertain whether or not you really had it so the doctor just had to take your word for it. Perfect. The guys rehearsed cries of torment all afternoon but it was pretty clear that Howard and Trev would never get away with it and so Luke performed for all the doctors and got certificates in three different names. He was so convincing that the last doctor insisted on giving him a morphine injection to put him out of his misery. It was the best stone he'd ever had. He was still flying on an hallucinogenic high the next day when he sat the legal ethics exam and he was ecstatic when he came out. He reckoned it was probably the most lucid and enlightening work he had ever produced.

He failed outright. It would be another year before he could graduate. Howard and Trev passed everything with flying colours, including the post, and began the new year as article clerks. I was appointed as an English teacher in a large inner-city high school.

I bought a new wardrobe of dresses and skirts and arrived excited and enthusiastic to meet my new colleagues. It was nothing like St George. The women wore slack-suits or sundresses and looked tired and depressed. The men wore Leisuremaster trousers with sewn-in creases or bermuda shorts with Parker pens tucked in long socks. They looked tired and depressed. The headmaster was drunk. They ate lunch from Tupperware boxes and drank instant coffee from their individually sloganned mugs— TEACHERS DO IT WITH CLASS. In the first week I learnt everything about teaching that I was ever likely to need.

1. The most important person in the school is not the headmaster but the headmaster's secretary. No one is more aware of this than the secretary herself.

2. The second most important person is not the deputy but the canteen lady.

3. The most boring person is the maths master or mistress who will fight constantly with all staff members but especially with the representative of the Teachers' Federation. The fed rep will have a beard, teach social sciences and hate teaching. He will talk daily of his latest plan 'to get out'.

4. The most ugly person is the PE teacher who will parade throughout the day in tiny running shorts, convinced that he is, in fact, the most attractive person. He is devoted to the promotion of sexism and adheres to the old adage, 'Spare the rod, create the poofter'.

6. Male staff will play ping-pong during all free periods and the female staff will watch.

7. Nobody on the staff ever thought that teaching would be like this.

Inside the classroom it was the survival of the fittest and one look at my senior classes left me in no doubt as to who that was. Every one of my pupils was bigger than me. They were stronger too and probably more sexually experienced, if the drawings on the desks were anything to go on. The girls sat at the front of the room with big, developed breasts and uniforms that just reached over their bottoms. The boys sat up the back, faces dark with after-five shadows and legs, too long to fit under desks, splayed out into the aisles. Trousers strained at the crotch and muscles bulged from short-sleeved shirts. The rooms were hot and overcrowded and pregnant with sex.

These 'kids' would just sit there and dare me to surprise them. I'd try. They'd wait. Within a month, every writer in the history of English literature was deemed by the group to be either boring, a homo or 'up himself'. Jane Austen was written off as a frustrated old maid who 'needed one'. I introduced my favourite poems and watched them wilt under apathy. I tried to motivate using Miss Pickwright's old system of badges but these kids had shirts covered with their own badges and a black cat was no match for 'SCHOOL SUX'. I persevered, remembering Mum's words.

'Teaching is lovely for a girl. You can always go back to it.'

But would you want to?

I wasn't brave enough to resign and anyway I needed the money. Luke and I had decided to move out of the hovel and buy our first home. He had become a car salesman while he waited to resit his exam at the end of the year. He wore a suit and a university tie for the men and his contact lenses for the women. His silver tongue flowed seductively, earning huge commissions and the title of Salesman of the Month three times running. He talked 'deals' and 'pitches' and 'closes' with the same ardour as he had recently talked Keats and Shelley and Yeats. The passion was the same, only the subject had changed. I was so proud of him. I knew he was winning his private struggle towards normalcy. And if I did sometimes regret the waning of the romantic and exotic, I knew it didn't have to be forever. Luke said it was all about creating a 'real asset base'. There were just certain things you had to do to get established. Deep down, the poetry could never die.

I wanted to buy in Glebe and took Luke back to Richmond Street. It was really changed. Most of the old residents had been removed long ago in the ultimate of disappearing acts, compulsory goverment relocation. And my dream of transforming one of the ugly little terraces was obviously not unique. Everyone was doing it. Backyard toilets had been converted into wine cellars, floors were covered with cork tiles and the hanging baskets swayed from every second balcony. The prices were way out of our range.

The old dark-brick semidetached cottage in Bondi was a real find. It was described by the bank's valuer as 'Plain and unattractive exterior. Interior: pokey and dark. Close to shops, schools and synagogue.'

It was in a good area, though, and Luke said there

were just three golden rules to real estate. Position, position, position. He said it was better to get the worst house in the best street than the best house in the worst street.

Amazingly enough, Dad agreed with him. Luke and I were visiting Bexley together these days. Mum had called a truce after Dad's first heart attack and now that Luke was in his new job, he was proving to be 'not such a bad bloke', after all. He didn't even take his commission when Dad traded in the old truck for a new Holden Statesman. Mum and Dad didn't dwell on the sexual reality of Luke and I living together. With Dad so sick, the question of my virginity paled into insignificance. I told them we had a bedroom each and the house was just an investment. And they believed me. Or decided to. But they never visited without ringing first.

The day we moved in we had a special tree-planting ceremony at the back fence. Luke picked the tree himself. It was the fastest growing species of gum in the world and he said it would mask the synagogue in no time. Trev and his new girlfriend brought over a bottle of champagne. Trev was really happy for us and was buying a place himself on the North Shore. It was all working out perfectly.

I loved being alone with Luke and having something we could work towards together. After school I cooked elaborate French food and we started giving small dinner-parties, with cloth serviettes and fresh flowers and three different types of cheese, for other couples. Luke joined the wine club. It's like that when you get your own place. You want to do things properly. And after years of trying, I finally knew how.

We shared all the housework. Luke knew the hip phrases for feminism and sexual discrimination but he knew far less about how to put them into practice. It wasn't his fault. His mother never dreamt her son would grow up in a world needing to know how to clean a toilet. It was inconceivable and a cruel twist of fate.

He assumed responsibility for the bathroom, regarding it as an exercise in time efficiency. He would come home from the car dealership on Fridays, strip to his undies and charge into the bathroom with a canister of Ajax in each hand. Then he'd run amok, shaking the tubes like maracas and letting the Ajax fly all over the floor, basin, toilet, bath and himself. Two minutes. Then he'd run into the garden, pull the hose through the window and spray the entire region at once. Two minutes. With a sponge in each hand he'd scrub all surfaces. Two minutes. Then he'd hose the lot once again before hopping in the shower for a rinse himself. The amount of water flooding the room never worried him. He insisted his method was based on the original design features. Why else would there be a little drain in the middle of the floor? His best time was eight and a quarter minutes. Occasionally it would stretch to ten if he decided to wash the dog at the same time. Shylock would be locked in the shower recess with the water running and then encouraged to shake the waterlogged fleas on to the floor before the final hosing. I found the whole procedure a bit unorthodox but I never said anything. I enjoyed Luke's new domesticity but I wanted the old flashes of insanity more.

The house was pretty much in its original 1935 condition except for little touches from the 1960s, like the false plaster fireplace in the lounge room. We planned to leave things as they were, for the time being. Luke's idea was to reduce our debts and then work on the house when he was a full-time solicitor. But I was impatient. One night, when we were stoned, I revved him up about how much we could do without spending very much money. I gave an impassioned speech about the value of aesthetics and finished the whole thing off by pointing at the fireplace, 'And that will be the first to go!'

He jumped up and raced to the laundry for a sledgehammer. He slammed it straight through the fireplace. I applauded. He slammed it again so there could be no going back in the morning. I applauded. We held each other in the debris and laughed. A long crack started to open in the wall in front of our eyes. It ran from the ceiling to the floor and back again. The renovations had irrevocably begun.

We scraped and sanded and painted for months. Luke would come home at night and pick up a paint brush before he put down his briefcase. He was a man possessed. He could describe our progress to the other salesmen by showing them his shirts which looked more like Dulux colour charts. The spot on the cuff was the Arctic Blue of the bedroom. The grey on the collar was the lounge room ceiling. We talked about nothing but how great it would be when it was finished.

And then it was. We sat out the back in the Peach Coral sunroom and bathed in our perfect achievement. Well, almost perfect. The tree-planting had proved to be the only disappointment. Not that the tree didn't grow quickly. It did. It had shot up fifteen feet, just as Luke had predicted. He just hadn't envisaged it to be fifteen feet of trunk. It was as if we had planted a telegraph pole with the intention of cutting the synagogue view in two. We sat looking at the trunk and the days began to drag. Now that the house was ready we had nothing to do. What next?

Let's get married!

It was a radical decision, a courageous *avant garde* act. No one else was doing it. Our friends were shocked. Mum and Dad were relieved. Rhonda and Sue were disappointed. It looked as if 'little sister' had taken the bait. I would do what my big sisters had done, after all. I didn't see it like that; we weren't bowing to social pressure. If anything, we were flying in the face of current social expectation. The days flew by again, filled with planning.

A lot of water had passed under the bridge since the Frangipani Lounge and I had very definite ideas about the way I wanted things to be. For a start, there would be no church and no reception. No hire cars. No brandy crustas. We wanted lunch for family and intimates in the garden of an Italian restaurant and a big party at the Bondi love nest that night. We could have a celebrant and exchange vows in a park beside the harbour. Mum and Dad offered to pick up the tab and went along with most of our plans. Dad was set on having the hire cars, though, and I had to spend my 'last night' at home. He wouldn't budge

Rhonda and Sue stayed the night as well. We watched the telly and painted our nails and cooked toasted sandwiches in the vertical grill. Dad listened to the trots in the kitchen and clapped his hands and danced a jig after a long shot, Pretty Princess, came in by a head. We took to our old beds, laughing about how strange and small they felt and joining in the old chorus of 'Goodnight, God bless, see you in the morning' from the dark corners of our rooms. Just like the old days. And, just like the old days, Mum was the last to fall asleep, saying our prayer, for all of us, out loud. 'Gentle Jesus, meek and mild, Look upon this little child...'

'I bags the shower after Rhonda.'

'No, your father's after Rhonda, then there's Sue.'

'Well, I bags the shower after Rhonda, after Dad and after Sue.'

Luckily, Mum had got up early to get hers over and done with before the rush. She was in her brunch coat with talcum powder caught in the folds of her bosom and new shoes pinching her toes. She was all dressed, bar her dress. After the queue for the bathroom, there was a fight for the iron and a jostle for the mirror. And then I was done. Rhonda snapped the Polaroid, Mum handed me a bouquet and Dad took my arm and said, 'Well, I've got to give it to you. You look beautiful, love.'

All the neighbours waited in the driveway to have a squizz. So that's why Dad insisted on the limo! There were some old school friends there too, including Chris Shackleton who had the baby in a stroller and looked as if she was pregnant again. She hugged me and cried and pressed a pair of baby bootees into my hand.

The celebrant was a swish woman with blond hair coiled high on her head and stilettos that kept sinking into the grass. She looked a lot like one of those ladies who sell cosmetics over a microphone in David Jones. Her name was Sue Anne Lovell and she smiled incessantly. She was good at her job, though, and she gathered the motley crew together in no time. This wasn't easy. Past and present mingled uneasily with pink crimplene dresses and Oroton handbags on one side and Lloyd Lomas haircuts and Flamingo Park cardigans on the other.

'Good friends, please, come closer. We will witness vows of love between Moya and Luke.'

Then she said something about us choosing the harbour instead of a church because we believed it was God's greatest cathedral. This wasn't true at all. We just thought it would look nice in the photos. Dad handed me to Luke. His silver tongue quivered as he gave his pledge.

'Moya, I promise to respect your rights as a free woman, to uphold your personhood in all its unique individuality. I promise to care for you forever or until such time as one of us feels it best (for their own development) to move on. For unlove is also a kind of love and has its place. As we are born into the cosmos, so we must be reborn.'

I didn't exactly understand all that Luke said but I think I made a similar commitment. Trev recited some verses from 'Desiderata' and Howie sang a Joe Cocker song, 'You are so beautiful' and that was it. The ceremony took seven minutes (including Sue Anne's bit about the harbour) and it was all over.

It was a fabulous day. The good thoughts and generosity of the group filled Luke and me with a strength and certainty that we had never felt before. Life stretched ahead like a dream, just made for us.

The caravan park at Forster may not have been everyone's idea of an idyllic honeymoon destination but it was all we could afford. Mum and Dad had a permanent site up there with all mod cons and very close to the amenities block. The lady in the office had filled the van with flowers and pinned a 'Just Married' sign on the annex. It was a good holiday, apart from the rain, but we couldn't wait to get back to the love nest to talk to our friends about the big day and look at the photos and start our new life afresh.

We were happy and just a bit smug too, I suppose. It's like that when you get married. Somehow you feel as if you've got something no one else has; that you've made yourselves safe.

We settled back into our day-to-day lives pretty quickly. I started teaching again and Luke was an article clerk. And then, a fortnight later, I came home from school and stopped dead in my tracks. Something was wrong in the kitchen. I saw Luke's new wedding shoes were on the table. It was *déjà vu*. They were lying there just like Rhonda's sling-backs had been lying on the table in Bexley years before. I sat down to take stock. And remembered.

I saw Mum crying in the old TV room. Rhonda's in trouble. I saw Dad in shock, his head in his hands.

Not Rhonda. Not Rhonda.

New shoes on the table.

What ill fortune would they bring this time?

Luke?

I put the kettle on.

Tragedy would find us in the love nest soon enough.